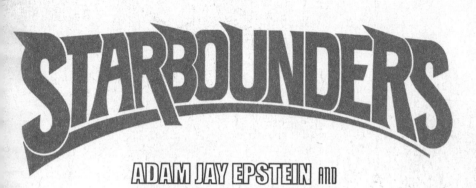

STARBOUNDERS

ADAM JAY EPSTEIN and ANDREW JACOBSON

HARPER

An Imprint of HarperCollinsPublishers

For Brian and Scott,
who are so much more than brothers to me.

And for Billy,
the older brother I never had.

—A. J. E.

For Ryder, Sam, and Nate,
the next generation of Jacobsons.

—A. J.

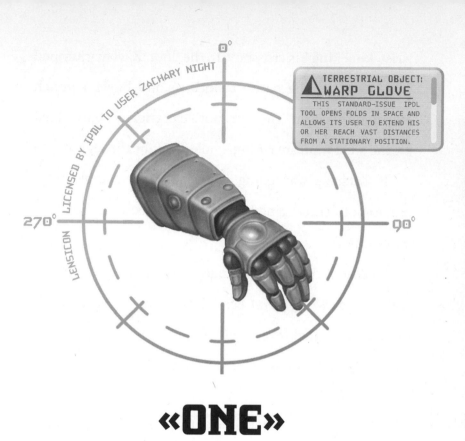

TERRESTRIAL OBJECT:
WARP GLOVE

THIS STANDARD-ISSUE IPDL TOOL OPENS FOLDS IN SPACE AND ALLOWS ITS USER TO EXTEND HIS OR HER REACH VAST DISTANCES FROM A STATIONARY POSITION.

«ONE»

Zachary moved swiftly then stopped, pressing his back up against a steel wall. He stood motionless, his index finger hovering above the trigger of his handheld sonic crossbow. In the silence, even the slightest breath of an approaching enemy could be heard. There was just one problem: robots didn't breathe.

Suddenly from around the corner a com-bot—a humanoid battle robot—appeared and kicked Zachary's wrist, knocking his crossbow to the floor. Zachary jumped back, avoiding the battle robot's second blow, a punch aimed for his head. The com-bot's electrically charged fist hit the steel wall, smashing a hole straight through it.

If Zachary was going to successfully complete his mission of neutralizing the system defenses, he'd have to move faster.

Undeterred, the robot lunged, snaring Zachary's wrist with its sparking metal claw. Immediately Zachary felt the current shock every nerve ending below his elbow, and his nostrils were flooded with the sulfurous odor of burned arm hair.

Zachary stretched his free hand to grab the sonic crossbow off the floor and took aim. He pulled the trigger, and a focused beam of sound struck the com-bot, blasting off the arm that was gripping his wrist. The robot reached out with its other claw and snagged the sonic crossbow, crushing it.

Zachary treaded backward, unintentionally cornering himself. With a snap, the com-bot's wrist compartment opened, revealing a set of whirling blades. Not eager to be sliced open like a can of tuna, Zachary dived between the com-bot's legs, rolling toward its disembodied arm and snatching it up. He swung the still-sparking claw, striking the chest of the com-bot and frying it instantly.

Zachary ran for the access panel that would disable the system defenses. He began to input the thirty-digit binary code that he'd been supplied in his mission brief when a voice called out from a speaker on the wall. "Wrap it up down there, Zachary. Dinnertime."

"Okay, okay," Zachary shouted. "Coming."

He went back to inputting numbers when the voice called again. One word: "Now!"

Zachary left the com-bot still smoking in a heap on the floor and headed up the stairs. Pushing open the trap-door in the ceiling, he climbed into his family's two-car garage and walked out to the driveway.

Zachary stopped to take it all in. Kids were riding down the sidewalk on bicycles and playing catch in the street. The smell of summer barbecue drifted over a nearby fence. He grinned to himself. Out here in the sub-urbs of Maryland, nobody knew that com-bots or sonic crossbows even existed. And they definitely had no idea that there was a Starbounder training simulator hidden underneath their neighbor's garage.

°°°

Zachary's sister, Danielle, was sitting on the living room floor with game controller in hand. She was playing one of the many space-combat games she had grown to be an expert in. Enemy aircraft exploded on the screen as she blasted her way through the game's futuristic skyline, but there was no sound coming from the TV. Danielle must have seen Zachary's reflection, because she paused the game and turned toward him.

You want to go head-to-head? she signed.

"And humiliate you one last time before I leave?" Zachary said, signing at the same time. "Absolutely."

He hopped over the couch and sat beside her, snatching up a controller in his hand. Zachary's dad stepped out from the kitchen.

"You can save the sibling smackdown for after dinner," he said and signed. "Now come set the table."

The two stood up with a sigh.

It's going to be quiet around here without you, Danielle signed to Zachary. *Well, more so,* she added with her typical deadpan humor.

Danielle had been born with 85-percent hearing loss, and by the time she turned nine, that had increased to 95 percent. The cause was never determined, and even the most advanced hearing aids couldn't help. To communicate with Danielle, the entire Night family had learned sign language, and the house had been tricked out with vibrating alarm clocks, and telephones and doorbells that set off strobe lights.

I'll be home for winter break in a few months, Zachary told her.

They entered the kitchen, where his dad was stirring sauce on the stove and his mom was straining pasta over the sink.

I still don't know why I can't go to Indigo 8, Danielle signed. *It's not fair.*

Zachary had thought the same thing when he was her age. But he didn't have to worry about that anymore. He'd be leaving for Indigo 8 in the morning. A secret compound hidden within the Adirondack Mountains, it was an earthbound base of operations for the Inter Planetary Defense League, or IPDL for short. It was also the place where Starbounders-in-training were taught the skills needed to protect the galaxy from outerverse threats.

Zachary would be spending the next five years of his life there, foregoing high school in favor of a different kind of education—one that would take him to places he had only dreamed about. Looking at Danielle's face, Zachary tried not to gloat, but he could hardly wait to get there.

Zachary's distant ancestor, Frederick Night, was one of the very first Starbounders. Generations of Nights followed, all the way down to Zachary's parents and older brother, Jacob. Knowing his great-great-grandfather was a hero and his brother was a big shot made Zachary proud. He never doubted his ability to follow in their footsteps. Much.

"I neutralized a com-bot programmed to lethal," Zachary told his parents as he grabbed a stack of plates from the cupboard.

"What you've learned down there is preschool compared to what's coming," Zachary's mom said. "Just remember, there's far more in this universe that you *don't* know than you do."

"Mom, I've been waiting my whole life for this," Zachary said. "I'm ready."

"Can I make a suggestion, Son?" Zachary's dad asked. "After dinner, before you finish packing and turn in for bed, take your bike out for one last spin around the neighborhood. Believe it or not, you're going to miss this place."

Which part? Zachary wondered. The single-lane bowling alley? The old movie theater playing the same film for months on end? Or the Dairy Queen where he and his friends would hang out on "exciting" nights?

No, something told him he wasn't going to miss Kingston at all.

That night he had a hard time sleeping. The clock by his bed read 11:15 as he forced himself to shut his eyes, only to open them again minutes later. A digital picture frame his mom had hung on the wall showed a continuous slideshow of photos, and as he tossed and turned through the night, he opened his eyes to see himself in numerous scenes: casting a line while fishing on the Delaware River, building a model rocket in his backyard, wearing an Indigo 8 cap three sizes too big for his head. In just a few hours he'd be leaving to go there. He wouldn't know another soul. Everything would be different than it was at home. No wonder he couldn't sleep.

Finally morning came. The duffel bag was tossed in the trunk, Danielle was dropped off at a friend's house, and Zachary and his parents were on their way. Six hours later, Zachary was sitting in the backseat staring out the window as his mom inched up a winding dirt road.

"Mom, could you be going any slower?" Zachary asked.

"You do realize who you're talking to, right?" Zachary's dad replied. "They used to call her Breakneck back when she was piloting spaceships."

"It's true," Zachary's mom said. "The reason you love fast things—go-karts, roller coasters, skateboarding down the roof of the school gym . . . You got that from me."

Zachary's mom pulled the car into the gravel lot of what looked like a deserted park. Zachary and his mom found a picnic table and began unpacking sandwiches from a cooler when his father excitedly handed Zachary a mahogany box.

"I wanted to give you this before we got there," he said.

Zachary put the mahogany box on the table and opened it to discover a metal orb the size of a tennis ball, with green and silver concentric circles looping around its surface. Looking closer, he could see a pulsing yellow light within the sphere.

"My own warp glove?" Zachary asked, wide-eyed.

"It *is* the most essential tool of any Starbounder," his dad said.

Zachary had seen Jacob's glove many times before, but he knew from an early age that their use was not permitted anywhere on Earth besides Indigo 8. He reached in and gripped the ball tight, instantly feeling the warm light against his skin and the cool metal on his fingertips.

"It belonged to your grandfather," Zachary's dad added. "That's the glove he was wielding during the Battle of Siarnaq. Under his command, a small Starbounder battalion defeated over a thousand Clipsians."

"But it's been resynched to your genome code," Zachary's mom said, interrupting a story Zachary had heard often. "Only your hand will be able to use it now."

"Squeeze it with your thumb and pinkie," his dad instructed.

As Zachary tightened his grip, the sphere split apart. A metal band extended out from the ball and snapped around his wrist like a handcuff. The metal continued to stretch across Zachary's skin, enveloping everything from the tips of his fingers all the way to his forearm. He could feel the gelatinous substance inside rippling around his wrist and hand. For a moment he imagined that it was his grandfather gripping his arm.

"How exactly does a warp glove work?" he asked.

"I don't pretend to understand the science of it, but basically it rips holes in the fabric of space itself," his dad said, taking a seat on the bench. "It's as if the universe we know is a bedsheet with wrinkles and folds. And instead of following along the surface of the sheet from one end to the other, it's like taking a shortcut through the folds."

Zachary continued to gaze at his right forearm, encased in the green-and-silver metallic glove. The slick exterior of the strange glove made it look stiff, but in fact it was just the opposite. He had full movement of his wrist and all of his fingers. There were pea-sized holes on each fingertip, and when he peered inside one he could see stars whirling and galaxies forming. It was almost as if the tiny hole was a window into the cosmos.

Zachary lifted his arm into the air and moved it about, up and down, left to right. He couldn't believe how flexible the glove was.

"Careful where you point that thing," Zachary's mom said. "You don't want to accidentally cause a black hole and swallow up everything within thirty miles."

"To take it off, just twist the sensor to the right," his dad said.

Zachary found the small silver button near his wrist and deactivated the glove. Before putting it back in the box, he held the orb in his hand and was struck by how heavy it was. He wasn't sure if the weight was from the metal itself or from the expectations that came with it.

° ° °

About an hour later the car rolled over a small bridge and passed a sign that read PINE LAKE ACADEMY. Through the woods, Zachary spotted a shimmering lake and ivy-covered brick dormitories. His mom drove past the quad, where some students were in the middle of a Frisbee game and others were reading beneath shady trees.

"This is Indigo 8?" Zachary said.

"No, this is just the cover," his mom replied as a girl dressed in a uniform crossed the road directly in front of their car.

"Mom, look out!" Zachary cried.

But his mom didn't stop. She didn't even slow down. Instead, she smashed right through the girl.

Zachary did a one-eighty and looked out the back window to see the girl continue on her way.

"What just happened?" he asked.

"Those aren't real students," his mom said. "They're called doppelforms. Holographic simulations of kids."

"Over a thousand laser projectors have been carefully placed around Pine Lake, mounted in trees and on roof-tops," Zachary's dad explained. "They're able to holograph-ically display students all over the campus. Employing an algorithm based on each individual's body mass index, bone density, and unique brain composition, Indigo 8's mainframe calculates how the doppelforms will interact within randomly generated lifelike scenarios."

"So what you're saying is that it's a real-life *Sims*," Zachary said. "You guys never told me about a cover."

"There's a lot we haven't told you," Zachary's dad said.

His mom drove past the science buildings, past the athletic field, and deeper into the woods, until the road came to a dead end at a mountain wall. She rolled down her window, and a trio of what looked like dragon-flies buzzed inside the car. As one flew close to his face, Zachary could see that it was a robot, with thin thermo-plastic wings, microscopic circuits running down its back, and a syringe-like tail. It landed on Zachary's neck, and he could feel a sharp metal needle graze against his skin, searching until it found a vein. Then there was a quick jab as the needle pierced his flesh. He was about to smack the dragonfly with his hand when it took to the air, its slen-der tail now filled with drops of his blood. Having taken samples from Zachary, his mom, and his dad, the three dragonfly inspectors flew back out the window, and a tun-nel through the mountain wall was revealed. Zachary's mom began to drive once more. A short distance later, the car emerged from the tunnel into a crater-shaped valley.

Ahead, Zachary could make out a lake and trees, but instead of brick buildings there were honeycomb-shaped structures lining the water. Their sides were covered in reflective solar paneling that glinted in the sun.

Farther away was a four-story tower that was narrow at the bottom but got wider as it rose up into the sky. Its top level rotated slowly. Standing majestically above it all was a clear cube. Cupping his hands into a telescope, Zachary peered inside. Staircases and ladders were leading up, down, and across in a way that started making him dizzy.

This was the real Indigo 8.

○ ○ ○

On their way to the bottom of the valley, they passed a football-field-sized archery range. Aerial targets were being launched into the sky, and Starbounders-in-training were shooting at them with bows loaded with what looked like beams of light.

"Look," Zachary's dad said excitedly. "The old starchery range. I was a pretty good shot in my day."

Zachary was still trying to take it all in, when his mom reached the parking lot. Across the pavement was a low, wide building with a reflecting pool out front. At the pool's center was a fountain in the shape of a figure eight spouting liquid metal that looked like silver—or mercury from an antique thermometer. Two empty buses were already parked in the lot, and resident advisors stood with tablets directing the new trainees to their sleeping quarters.

Now that it was time for Zachary to join them, his feet felt heavy.

His dad walked around to the trunk and pulled out Zachary's duffel bag, while his mom rummaged through her purse and looked under the passenger seat.

Zachary glanced up at the clear cube structure he had spotted during their descent into the valley. Now he could clearly see kids floating inside, as if gravity had no effect on them. Some were gliding headfirst down from the top to the bottom; others were somersaulting diagonally upward. Two teenagers were sparring on an upside-down staircase with flexible combat sticks. Others were playing some sort of midair game of handball on the ladders, slapping a green, spongy sphere off the ceiling at blur-inducing speeds.

Zachary's dad set the bag down with a thump.

"Toothpaste," Zachary's mom said, bursting out of the car. "I forgot to pack it."

"That's why they have vending machines," his dad said, placing a gentle hand on his mom's shoulder. "Why don't we let Zachary take it from here?"

"We'll help him get settled," his mom said. "I can put

the sheets on his sleeping pod."

"He's a Night, sweetheart. He'll manage."

Zachary's mom nodded.

Zachary reached down for his bag, but it wasn't there. He turned to see that it was already being lifted by the mechanical tendrils of something that looked like a hovering jellyfish. Depositing the bag into its transparent belly, the automated porter zipped off down the hill.

"Did that robot just steal my duffel bag?"

Zachary's dad let out a laugh. But his mom had a serious expression on her face. She walked over and gave Zachary a hug.

"Just promise me you'll be safe."

"I promise," Zachary said, feeling his mom gripping him tighter than usual before she finally let go and stepped back. As she did, a female resident advisor in a tank top approached Zachary with tablet in hand.

"First year here?" she asked.

"Is it that obvious?" Zachary replied, looking at the galaxy of stars tattooed on her arm.

The resident advisor smiled. "Just step on the pathway, and Cerebella will guide you to your SQ."

Now Zachary noticed the black glass sidewalks that stretched out from the parking lot and wound their way all through the campus, snaking around the well-manicured lawns.

Zachary turned back to his mom and dad. He had so much to say, but what he settled on was, "Oh, I almost forgot. Make sure Danielle stays out of my room."

And with that, Zachary walked up to one of the pathways, its slick surface resembling the touch screen of a smartphone. He paused. Though he would only be taking one small step forward, he knew it would be the start of his own daring voyage into the unknown.

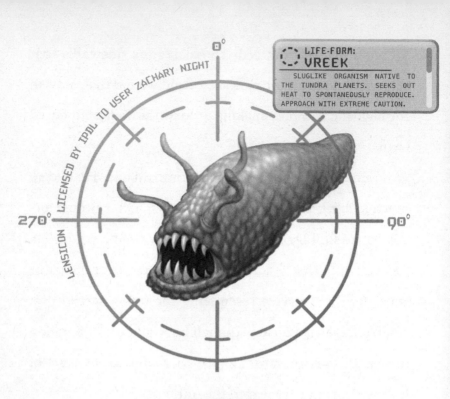

0°

270°

90°

LIFE-FORM:
VREEK
SLUGLIKE ORGANISM NATIVE TO
THE TUNDRA PLANETS. SEEKS OUT
HEAT TO SPONTANEOUSLY REPRODUCE.
APPROACH WITH EXTREME CAUTION.

«TWO»

"Welcome, Zachary Night," a pleasant female voice said as his foot hit the surface. "Let me guide you to your sleeping quarters."

A neon-green line appeared on the pathway, stretching all the way toward one of the honeycomb structures at the far west end of the hill. Following the green line, Zachary set off on the cross-campus trek. He looked out at the nearby lake and watched as several small boats with oversized translucent sails zipped across it even though there wasn't the slightest bit of wind to propel them.

Zachary was still trying to figure out how the boats were moving—could it have been the sunlight?—when he spotted a four-legged, two-armed creature moving toward him on the pathway from the other direction. It stood over six feet tall and was wearing a white rubber suit that clung to its leathery tan skin. Definitely not human, it had a face that looked like an anteater's. Two glass canisters filled with orange vapor were strapped to its neck, with clear tubes extended out from them and looping into the corners of the alien's mouth like bent straws. With each breath, it sucked in orange smoke from the canisters and let it out through the tubes.

"Good afternoon, young Starbounder. I am Instructor Yiddagog." The creature's voice entered Zachary's brain as clearly as if the words had been spoken aloud. But they hadn't been. Zachary was tongue-tied. He'd never seen a living alien before, let alone one that could send messages directly into his mind. "It's customary to respond to a greeting. Even if that greeting is delivered telepathically."

"H-Hello," Zachary said, stuttering out the two syllables.

"Hello, indeed," the alien said (or thought?). It continued on, its clawed toes pulling it forward and wisps of orange smoke trailing behind. The vapors got up Zachary's nose and acted like pepper. He wasn't sure how long he'd been standing there sneezing before the pleasant female voice from the black sidewalk called out to him.

"Please resume normal foot speed. The Lightwing Boys' SQ is just fifty-two yards away. Your presence is required there."

Close up, the honeycomb buildings were almost blinding to look at, with the sun reflecting off every angle of their mirrored exteriors. Zachary didn't stop until the pathway led him right up to the six-sided door of his sleeping quarters. He reached out to knock, but before his knuckles made contact, it opened automatically. Zachary passed through. His hairs began to stand on end as though he'd rubbed his socks on the carpet in his living room and then touched a metal door handle. An electric field? What for? Zachary wondered.

Inside, the sleeping quarters looked like the interior of a spaceship—at least the ones Zachary had seen in video games and movies—with silver trim and gray padded floors and ceilings. The beds—pods shaped like eggshells halved lengthwise—were built into the walls and stacked three high. Most of them were already taken, with sheets and pillows thrown on messily. More than a dozen boys Zachary's age were unpacking their duffels and trunks, removing socks, tees, and an assortment of unusual outerverse devices, from strange-looking tweezers with balls on the ends instead of points to pitch-black life jackets with small booster rockets strapped around the torso.

A red-haired boy with a sunburn was starting to put on one of the vests and must have accidentally activated it. He got pulled off his feet as the vest launched from his fingers and zipped across the room. The flying jacket bounced off a sleeping pod and crashed into a lanky kid's trunk, sending his belongings spilling out.

"Watch it, Chuck," the boy said. "There's a reason you're not supposed to wear those inside."

"My bad," Chuck said, his face getting even redder.

Another Lightwing boy standing nearby removed what appeared to be a retainer from his mouth, only it was embedded with sparkling diodes.

"Hey, Apollo, hear anything interesting?" one of his

bunkmates called from across the SQ.

Hear? thought Zachary.

"All six hundred bands are covering the Clipsian attack on the Tranquil Galaxies," Apollo said. "I'd like to see those charcs take on the IPDL instead of starbombing unarmed planets."

"We don't use that kind of language around here," a voice bellowed from behind.

Apollo scoffed and continued unpacking.

The voice belonged to an Asian man, who looked to be in his midtwenties. He wore a T-shirt with an infinity logo on it.

"How would you like it if an off-planet called you a *red-blood*?" he asked.

"It takes more than that to hurt my feelings," Apollo said, removing a warp-glove box from his bag.

The man reached a hand out toward Zachary.

"I'm Kwan, one of your resident advisors."

"Zachary," he said, shaking Kwan's hand.

"I know. You look just like your brother. And if you're half as good a pilot as him, you'll be commanding an entire fleet of pitchforks before you're old enough to drive a car. Of course, you've got a mighty big glove to fill. Jacob was one of the youngest Starbounders ever to be recruited into the Elite Corps. Last I heard he was hunting Molking raiders in the Platurex Dominion."

"Just like Dad and Granddad before him, striking fear into the scum of the galaxy," Zachary said.

"That's Derek, your other resident advisor," Kwan said, gesturing to a smaller, out-of-shape guy with his nose buried in a tablet. "You have questions about spaceflight, combat, or campus regulations, you come to me. You have questions about girls, you go to Derek." Zachary looked over at Derek, then back to Kwan, surprised. "I'm just messing with you. You come to me about girls, too."

"Definitely not my area of expertise," Derek said, without looking up.

"You better find a bunk," Kwan said. "Unfortunately for you, it was first come, first served."

All that remained available were clearly the least appealing places to sleep in the SQ—a few top beds in the back corner over by the bathroom. Zachary spotted his duffel bag sitting alone in the center of the room, retrieved it, and headed for the unoccupied sleeping pods.

He passed by a kid with braces surrounded by a group of trainees. The kid was showing off a pair of metal wrist cuffs connected by a chain of pure electricity.

"They're called shockles," the kid said. "My dad was the warden of an asteroid prison. He never went to work without 'em."

Zachary reached the corner, slid his duffel bag into a storage space marked *top*, and began unpacking. He pushed aside his clothes and the mahogany box storing his grandfather's warp glove, then pulled out a pillow and sheets before climbing a ladder to the topmost pod just below the ceiling.

In a neighboring upper bunk, another trainee was making his bed. His appearance took Zachary by surprise. As human as the boy seemed, it was obvious that he wasn't: his skin and bald head were pale and veiny like a bloodshot eyeball, and his arms were a little longer and more rubbery than they should have been. The boy noticed Zachary staring at him.

"I'm Ryic," he said, laying a blanket covered in bristles over the mattress. "Ryic 1,174,831 to be exact. But you don't use birth numbers on your planet, do you?

You can just call me Ryic."

"Zachary."

"I'm one of the twelve outerverse exchanges," Ryic said. "My home planet doesn't have a Starbounder training academy."

"So you're, like . . . an alien?" Zachary asked.

"I could say the same thing about you."

Ryic had a point. Zachary reached out to shake his hand, but Ryic didn't even have to lean forward: his arm extended itself like Silly Putty out of his pod and across to Zachary. Ryic's skin felt like the outer peel of an orange, soft but slightly bumpy to the touch. His grip was surprisingly strong for someone so malleable.

"Where I come from, on Klenarog, gravity is significantly stronger, so in the course of the evolution of our species, our bodies became increasingly flexible to prevent our bones from breaking. The weaker gravity on Earth makes us even more elastic than usual."

As Ryic's arm retracted back to his pod, he said, "You're leaking." Zachary was confused. He looked down to see if he had spilled water on himself. "No, from your head."

Zachary put the back of his hand to his brow and

found a few beads of perspiration there. He wiped them away.

"That's just sweat," he said. "Humans get it when they're hot or exercising."

"How strange," Ryic said.

"Is that what you're going to sleep on?" Zachary asked, eyeing the quill-covered blanket.

"Oh, yes. I like my sheets prickly. And my pillows firm."

Ryic stretched an arm down to his duffel bag on the ground and removed a cinder block. He brought it up to the top pod and dropped it at the head of the bed with a loud thunk.

"Usually I prefer something harder, but this was all that would fit with my stuff."

Ryic reached back down, and this time, he pulled out a bag of what looked like green, sugarcoated candies.

Just as Ryic was about to take one of the treats, a black hole materialized inches away from the bag. A crimson-colored warp glove emerged from the hole and stole the bag. Zachary and Ryic looked down from their sleeping pods to see Apollo pulling Ryic's bag of candies out from another hole on the other side of the SQ. A millisecond later the black rupture in space disappeared.

"Hope you don't mind sharing," Apollo said with a cocky grin. Some of his bunkmates laughed as Apollo tossed a handful of the candies into his mouth.

"Interesting," Ryic said. "Most humans don't have a taste for Flobian roach brain."

Apollo immediately spit out the alien snack, wiping the green from his tongue. Suddenly, the laughter in the sleeping quarters turned on him.

"Attention all Lightwings," the soothing sidewalk voice said, only this time it came from the walls. "Report to the Ulam for your gravity test."

"All right, everyone, you heard Cerebella," Kwan said. "She doesn't ask twice."

Zachary and Ryic climbed down from their pods and joined the rest of their bunkmates as everybody headed for the door. When Zachary stepped over the threshold, he again felt the electric tingle.

"Keeps away mosquitoes," Derek said as he passed by.

It might have been a fine deterrent for bugs, Zachary thought, but it hardly seemed worth the goose bumps every time he walked in or out of the SQ.

Outside, the black sidewalk beneath Zachary's feet lit up with bright silver arrows pointing to the Ulam. Upon reaching the building by the parking lot, Zachary and the others walked up the semicircle of steps that led around the reflecting pool and mercury-filled fountain. They entered a large foyer walled in by smoked glass; the room's dark tint made Zachary feel like he was wearing sunglasses.

On one of the walls were hi-res satellite projections of the other Indigo bases from around the galaxy. There were dozens of them, some in daylight, others in darkness. Several were inhabited by human-looking Starbounders-in-training, but the majority appeared to be populated by creatures most definitely not of Earth.

When Zachary glanced up to the ceiling, he noticed that one of the glass panels that made up the top of the foyer displayed what looked like a traditional newscast, except that the anchor was not human but some kind of robot. The sound wasn't on, but images flashed by of alien farmers coping with floods, the launching of large space pods from bodies of water, and trident-shaped fighter ships with indigo stripes flying in formation.

On the far wall was a row of pedestals, each with a sculpture of a planet resting atop it. A plaque reading OUTERVERSE MEMORIAL hung above them. Inscribed on the pillars were brief histories of the planets and the date and circumstance of each one's destruction.

"We can't save them all," said Derek regretfully as he walked past.

Right at the center of the space was a three-dimensional holographic map of the entire building. Zachary stopped before it and, upon closer inspection, he could see just how big the Ulam was: this glass foyer was only the tip of the iceberg; most of the building's rooms and tunnels were below ground and not visible.

"I had no idea Indigo 8 was so big," Zachary said to Kwan, who had come up beside him. Derek and the rest of the Lightwings were already heading out of the foyer.

"Training future Starbounders is only a small part of what we do here," Kwan replied. "It's also a central defense base for the IPDL, so there's a strategic command center; a detention facility for off-planet criminals; and, fifty stories below us, a fleet of pitchforks and battle-axes ready to be deployed at a moment's notice."

"Wait, did you say the spaceships were underground?" asked Zachary.

"The spacecraft don't launch like traditional rockets into the sky," Kwan answered. "Instead, they slip through a fold in space that sends them to the dark side of Jupiter. That way they go undetected by Earth's telescopes. Hubble, Magellan, Gemini—none of them have any idea we exist. So government officials, scientists, and everyday people don't either."

Zachary had spent his life surrounded by those everyday people. His neighbors, his friends. Even his science teacher. All living in their small town of Kingston, never realizing that space travel to other galaxies was not only possible but happening all the time. And soon it would be Zachary's turn to make that trip.

"Come on," Kwan said. "We should catch up with the others."

Before Zachary took off, his eyes were drawn back to the holographic map of the Ulam. There on level three he spotted the Frederick Night Dimensional Strategy Center. He'd heard his family speak with pride about the center, but seeing his great-great-grandfather's name on the map just added to the pressure he already felt to excel at Indigo 8.

Zachary hurried ahead, imagining that one day part of the Ulam might bear his name, too. He caught up with Kwan, and found the rest of the group in a long hallway with massive glass terrariums built into the walls. Each recreated a different alien ecosystem and had vegetation and life-forms that were clearly not native to Earth. Zachary walked up beside Ryic, who had stopped to stare at a swamp of red plants and vines. Swimming circles in the murky puddle of water was a trio of creatures that resembled dreadlocked orange fish.

"Reminds me of my first pet," Ryic said.

"I had goldfish, too," Zachary said.

Just then, one of the three creatures exploded, sending pea-sized eggs all over the terrarium.

"Of course, none of my goldfish ever did that," Zachary said.

"Mine did," Ryic said. "There'll be lots more soon."

Ahead of them, at another terrarium, an overexcited trainee was slapping his palm to get the attention of whatever was inside. Zachary walked over to see a sluglike organism hidden among a patch of frost-encrusted flowers. The silvery-gray slug did an excellent job blending in with the icicle-covered thorny shrubs that filled the wintery habitat.

"Hey, hands off the glass," Derek said. "You like it when people shake your bed when you're trying to sleep?"

He had barely gotten the words out before the slug flung itself against the window at the boy's hand. The trainee jumped back as the creature bared a row of gnashing teeth and tried in vain to eat its way through the glass.

"Give that window a kiss," Derek said. "It just saved your right hand from a vreek."

The boy tucked his fingers into his pockets and shuffled away.

They kept moving until they reached a translucent tunnel that connected the Ulam to the ten-story-tall zero-gravity cube. The group entered a small holding room where around fifteen Lightwing girls were already waiting. Zachary's attention was drawn to two trainers who were gliding downward inside the cube, somersaulting through a series of rings and platforms that floated in midair.

The two trainers' boots landed squarely on the floor, and Zachary got a good look at them. The young man had inch-long black hair and a beard of equal length. He wore a skintight silver bodysuit and what looked like moon boots with some kind of rough Velcro tread on the bottom. The young woman was dressed in a matching outfit.

The male trainer pressed his thumb against a panel, and a glass door slid open, allowing him to pass through an antechamber before entering the holding room.

"I'm Loren." He gave an exaggerated bow. "Yes, I know, it sounds like a girl's name. My parents were convinced they were having a daughter, but they got me instead." The Lightwing boys and girls laughed. "We're going to split you into groups of four and see how you fare in the Qube. Suit up and find a pair of friction boots that fit you. Monica and I will be evaluating your skill level for training placement."

Zachary and the other boys and girls walked over to the far side of the tank, where rubber padded suits were hanging on hooks, and boots of all sizes sat in cubbies. He grabbed an outfit that looked about his height; it was long-sleeved with full-length pants. He then reached for a pair of size-seven boots, but it was as if they'd been glued down. He gave them a tug to pull the bottoms free from the cubby shelf. He tugged and tugged again, but the boots wouldn't give. Finally, he gave them a twist, and they released immediately.

And Zachary wasn't the only one struggling with the boots. Ryic was as well. When he finally dislodged a pair from the cubby, Ryic went stumbling back into a girl standing behind him. They both fell in a heap.

"First day on your new feet?" the girl asked.

Ryic looked at her curiously. "No, these are the same feet I have always had."

"Didn't anybody ever teach you how to put on a pair of Armstrongs before?" the girl asked Ryic.

Ryic looked at her curiously. So did Zachary.

"Armstrongs?" Zachary repeated.

"Nickname for friction boots," she said. "Named after that dude who first walked on the moon. Or at least the one everyone thinks did."

The girl had a blond pixie cut with dyed streaks of blue, three piercings in her left ear, and one in her right. She wore black knit stockings beneath a pair of jean shorts,

Converse high-tops, and a shirt with holes in it that had either gotten that way from years of wear or, more likely, had been bought with them.

Zachary stared at her a little bit longer than he intended to. He caught glimpses of the oversized rings on her fingers and the flower doodled on her forearm in glittery magenta.

"Take a picture, it'll last longer," she said. "If your mental photo needs a tag, I'm Kaylee."

"I'm Zachary. This is Ryic."

Kaylee didn't give much more than a shrug back in response.

Zachary slipped his foot into one of the friction boots, and as soon as his heel and toe were in place, the boot tightened around his ankle on its own. It was a snug fit, less comfortable than the warp glove. The only sensation he could compare it to was the time that a boa constrictor wrapped itself around his arm at a friend's birthday party.

Soon all the Lightwings were gathering in a semicircle around Loren and Monica, chattering excitedly.

"All right, let's start with you, you, you, and you," Loren said.

Realizing that the final *you* was directed at him, Zachary was hit with a surge of adrenaline. Since the day his parents had told him about Indigo 8, Zachary had been waiting for this moment. A chance to prove himself. And he wanted to experience zero gravity. Jacob had said there was nothing like the sensation of being weightless. Now Zachary would finally get to feel it for himself.

Lightwings who hadn't been chosen for the first round groaned, disappointed.

"Monica, why don't you take it from here," Loren said.

"Sure thing." Monica turned to Zachary, Kaylee, and the other two trainees chosen. "You'll all be competing against each other on the zero-gravity obstacle course. The object is to pass through the numbered rings in order. Today's race is noncontact, which means no hitting, pushing, or springboarding. If you unintentionally collide, just keep going. At the sound of the siren, begin."

Zachary sized up his competition: besides Kaylee there was Chuck, the red-haired kid with the sunburn from his SQ, and an eager brunette whose bunkmates had called her Cee Cee. Loren reopened the glass divide and led them into the Qube. Immediately, Zachary felt lighter. It reminded him of the sensation he got taking off his heavy school backpack after a long walk home. Zachary's arms, so used to hanging by his side, were drifting up on their own. The stickiness on the bottom of his friction boots was the only thing that kept him from lifting off.

The four Starbounders-in-training all lined up on an elevated portion of the floor, waiting for the siren to—

Beeeep!

Zachary bent his knees, twisted his boots, and jumped. Just like that, he was airborne. He felt like he was floating in a swimming pool, except there was no water. Chuck, a little weightier than the rest, had a more forceful take-off, catapulting himself to a quick lead. But speed wasn't the only factor in zero-gravity acrobatics; accuracy was equally important. The red-haired boy went soaring past the first ring, clipping one of the platforms and entering a freefall upward. Chuck didn't stop until his body slammed into the glass ceiling ten stories up, like a bug hitting the windshield of an oncoming car.

Out of the corner of his eye, Zachary saw all the Lightwings watching from the other side of the glass flinch in unison.

Zachary was the first to successfully complete ring one, vaulting himself like an arrow straight through the center. His eyes scanned the Qube for ring two and saw that it was back toward the bottom. Kaylee might not have been as fast, but she was obviously clever. She'd thought a move ahead. Instead of flying directly through ring one, she grabbed on to it and swung herself around so she was already heading down to the next. By the time Zachary spotted the second ring and readjusted course, Kaylee was already halfway there.

Zachary pushed off the upside-down staircase, launching himself in the opposite direction as he tried to catch up to Kaylee. Just then, Cee Cee flailed helplessly right into his path, flapping her arms like a wounded bird, getting absolutely nowhere.

"Watch out!" Zachary called.

Moments before making impact with her, Zachary barrel-rolled out of the way, his foot narrowly missing the top of her head as he continued downward. Kaylee glanced back over her shoulder as she passed through ring two.

"Go back to the monkey bars on the playground," she taunted Zachary. "This is where the big kids play."

He smiled, swinging himself through ring two and across the Qube again. As he and Kaylee soared toward ring three, Zachary glanced back through the translucent wall into the hallway where all of the other trainees were watching. Although he couldn't hear them through the soundproof glass, it appeared that the Lightwing boys and Lightwing girls were cheering on their respective bunkmates. Zachary didn't want to disappoint.

"How 'bout we make this interesting?" Zachary asked, closing the gap. "Loser does the winner's laundry for a week."

"Just so you know, I like my socks folded, not balled," Kaylee replied.

They passed through the third ring at the same time, their chests practically touching as they came out the other side.

The fourth, and final, ring was extra challenging. Unlike the first three, which remained stationary, this one moved in space unpredictably and also contracted and expanded at random intervals. Zachary realized it and knew he would have to time his entrance perfectly.

"Give up already," Kaylee called.

"The fumes from all that hair dye must be making you delusional," Zachary said. "I got this."

The two jockeyed for position down the homestretch, leaping from platform to platform. Zachary waited for the ring to contract before he gave himself one final push-off, knowing that by the time he reached it, the circle would have opened once more. As the ring expanded, Zachary soared toward his target. Kaylee was right there beside him.

Zachary's fingers crossed through the ring first, but Kaylee exited the other side less than a second before he did.

"Wow," Loren said. "A photo finish."

"Yeah, but Kaylee's the clear winner," Monica added.

Zachary and Kaylee floated down to the ground.

"Just for the record, my hand crossed that ring first," Zachary said.

"Well, too bad I beat you out the other side," Kaylee replied with a satisfied grin. "And the object is to get *through* the rings first."

"Oh, did you consult the international zero-gravity-obstacle-course rules committee?" Zachary asked.

"I did," she replied. "They said I won and you lost."

"I wasn't even close," Chuck said, joining them.

They were heading for the glass doors back into the hallway when Cee Cee called out from above.

"Would somebody get me down from here?" She was now upside down in midair, hanging like a piñata with no string. "I'm stuck!"

"Hang tight," Loren said. "I'm coming to get you."

Zachary watched as Loren sprang up from the platform, soaring three stories into the air. He grabbed Cee Cee by the hand, but before he was able to assist her with her descent, they both began to fall. They tumbled through the air so fast it was impossible for anyone to react. Zachary suddenly felt about a hundred pounds heavier. Gravity had unexpectedly returned to the Qube.

Just as quickly, the gravity glitch ended, and he felt weightless again, but it was too late. Loren and Cee Cee had already slammed into the ground. From behind the glass wall, Zachary could see that some of the other Lightwings quickly turned away, while others watched in horror.

Monica ran over to a speaker panel in the wall.

"We need EMA in the Qube. There's been a Cerebella malfunction."

"Medics are on their way," a voice called back.

Loren was gritting his teeth and holding his shoulder. Cee Cee was unconscious but breathing.

If that glitch had happened a minute sooner, Zachary would have been lying on the ground, too. Injured or worse. He knew how hazardous being a Starbounder could be, but he never imagined he would be dodging his first brush with death before dinner.

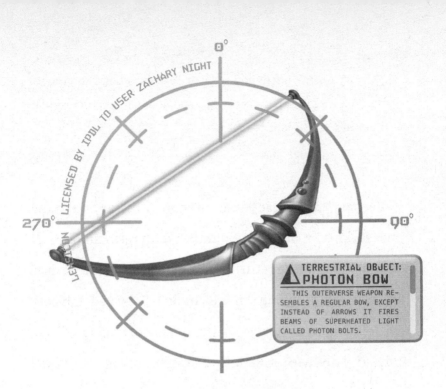

LICENSED BY IPDL TO USER ZACHARY NIGHT

LENGTH

0°

270°

90°

⚠ TERRESTRIAL OBJECT:
PHOTON BOW

THIS OUTERVERSE WEAPON RE-
SEMBLES A REGULAR BOW, EXCEPT
INSTEAD OF ARROWS IT FIRES
BEAMS OF SUPERHEATED LIGHT
CALLED PHOTON BOLTS.

«THREE»

LIGHTWING BOYS:

Week Two Schedule Changes

Monday:

Due to an inclement-weather forecast for the afternoon, the Chameleon game has been moved to 5:00 p.m. Please attend regular training classes after lunch.

Bonfire at the lake will follow the game.

○ ○ ○

Zachary had already read over the itinerary so many times he knew it by heart. So rather than torment himself with anticipation, he returned to the tactical flight manual he had been studying on his Indigo 8–issued tablet—which had been preloaded with course curricula and was updated daily with scheduling announcements. He was about to scroll through pitchfork flight patterns when Ryic hurried over, nearly out of breath.

"Zachary, I am deeply troubled. I witnessed an older female trainee administering mouth-to-mouth resuscitation to a male trainee, and yet no one around them seemed to be calling for medical assistance."

Zachary followed Ryic's worried gaze across the Skyterium to the pair in question. He couldn't see their faces because they were lip-locked, but he knew they were Darkspeeders—the oldest group of trainees—by the emblem of a flying motorcycle on the shoulders of their shirts.

"Ryic, that's called kissing."

"Will he be okay?" Ryic asked with genuine concern.

"Yeah, I think he's going to live—"

"The dwarf planet Pluto is now coming into focus," Cerebella's voice interrupted them.

Even though the hour before lights-out was meant for socializing, Indigo 8 didn't miss a teaching moment. The Skyterium was like a planetarium without seats, but instead of a projector displaying images of the universe on the ceiling, the entire roof of the building acted as a telescopic lens, bringing the stars and sky practically within reach. There was a snack bar on one side, and beanbag chairs scattered about. Cerebella's voice continued as Zachary glanced up to see the distant celestial object.

"Slightly smaller than the Earth's moon, this dwarf planet has an atmosphere composed mostly of nitrogen, methane, and carbon monoxide. Its severely cold temperatures reach two hundred thirty-three degrees below zero Celsius."

She had more to say, but Zachary turned his attention back to Ryic.

"Want to get a fruit punch?" Zachary asked.

"I still don't understand why you call this beverage fruit punch," Ryic said. "Is it made by pounding one's fists into various fruits?"

The two headed for the snack counter. Just as they arrived at the back of the line, they heard a raised voice from nearby.

"Well, I don't think you belong at Indigo 8. Not with what the Clipsians have been doing in the outerverse. Your people just ravaged the Tranquil Galaxies. How are we supposed to trust you when your kind doesn't respect IDPL law?"

Zachary turned to see that the voice belonged to Instructor Avendale, who taught his warp-glove-wielding class. She had a shock of white hair pulled back tightly in a ponytail and she never wore makeup. Her words were directed at Professor Excelsius Olari. Although Olari was roughly human in shape—torso, two arms, two legs—like all Clipsians, he had only one eye and a slit for a mouth, but no nose or ears. His skin resembled warm charcoal: an ashy black on the outside, with red embers glowing beneath. He oversaw Zachary's morphology course, where trainees learned about all the various alien life-forms that existed beyond Earth. Whenever Professor Olari got excited by what he was talking about, heat would radiate from his body, making his fingertips and forehead redden the same way burning charcoal did. That was why people like Instructor Avendale and Apollo called his kind charcs.

"I would have expected more from you, Lydia," Professor Olari said.

"I don't care if others won't say it out loud." Instructor Avendale ran a hand through her white hair, putting a single stray strand back in place. "How do I know we won't be next?"

"I deplore what Nibiru and his armada did to the Tranquil Galaxies. They are rogues," the Clipsian professor said. "I can assure you that the majority of our species is as peaceful as any other in the IPDL."

Zachary could see orange embers starting to glow brighter through the cracks of Professor Olari's skin.

"I'll be keeping an eye on you this year, Excelsius. Be warned."

Instructor Avendale walked away, leaving Professor

Olari seething and red in the face.

Kaylee walked up behind Zachary and Ryic.

"Of all the vile creatures in the universe, how did the worst end up at Indigo 8?" she asked.

"Perhaps you shouldn't judge Professor Olari so quickly," Ryic said.

"I was talking about Instructor Avendale. She's the dangerous one." Kaylee turned to Zachary. "I'm surprised to see you here. Don't you have some laundry you should be doing?"

"Come on, I've already done three loads for you. You're just torturing me now."

"The deal was you had to do my laundry for a week. And by my estimation there's still sixteen hours left, so you've got time for at least one more. My bag's right over there."

Zachary sighed and shook his head.

"Right now?"

"My favorite running shorts are in there, and we've got our first Chameleon game tomorrow," Kaylee said. "Chop-chop."

"Remind me never to make a bet with you again,"

Zachary said, heading for the laundry bag.

"Try not to accidentally mix the colors in with the whites this time," Kaylee called out.

"That wasn't an accident," Zachary shot back at her.

°°°

The laundry room was on the second basement level of the Ulam. It was rarely crowded, and Zachary figured it would be empty now, seeing as how everyone was still upstairs in the Skyterium. He lugged Kaylee's bag inside and was startled to find someone standing over the sink. It was Loren, the trainer from the Qube. His arm was still in a sling from the accident. He looked surprised to see Zachary, too.

"Hey, shouldn't you be upstairs with everyone else?" Loren asked.

"I'm still paying off that bet I lost to Kaylee," Zachary said.

Loren smiled.

"There's an empty machine by me," he said.

Zachary walked over and started loading Kaylee's laundry into the washer. He saw that Loren was scrubbing a knit green shirt with one hand.

"Chameleon jerseys," Loren said. "For tomorrow's game. It's like capture the flag meets laser tag."

"Yeah, my brother used to talk about it all the time." Then Zachary asked, "Can I help you there?"

"Nah, I'm getting pretty good at doing stuff one-handed," Loren said. "I was really impressed by your performance in the Qube last week. You're a natural."

"It kind of comes with the last name."

"I know how that is." Loren shut off the sink and put the jerseys in the dryer. "My father was an IPDL commander. Highly decorated, too."

"What for?" Zachary said.

"Dying with valor. His ship went down during a rescue mission. It wasn't even the crash that killed him, though. He sent out a distress call, but by the time the IPDL showed up, it was too late. His body couldn't adjust to the microorganisms in the planet's atmosphere. Total organ failure."

Zachary averted his eyes, not sure how to respond.

"I was only five when it happened. I didn't really know him. My mom always told me I could be angry about it and carry around a grudge my whole life, or I could honor my dad and carry out his legacy as a Starbounder. So here I am."

Zachary could certainly relate to carrying on a family legacy. His eyes returned to Kaylee's laundry bag.

"Is this a white or a color?" He held up a beige shirt.

"It's safer to go color," Loren said.

Zachary shoveled a sloppy cupful of detergent into the machine.

"So, any advice before tomorrow's game?" he asked.

"There's a reason they call it Chameleon. The best way not to get hit is not to be seen."

° ° °

The following afternoon, Zachary's purple jersey flapped in the wind as he raced through the woods on the outskirts of Indigo 8. A fellow Chameleon teammate ran at his side, puffing so hard it seemed as if he would faint at any moment.

The rules of the game were simple enough. All of the Starbounders-in-training were separated into four different teams. The first to collect a baton from each of the opposing teams and return all three to their base would win. To neutralize their opponents, every player wore a computer-controlled belt armed with five stun balls, which remained charged until they were plucked off and thrown. If a ball made contact with an opposing player, it emitted a shock that stunned him or her into temporary paralysis. The trainers claimed it was just a sting, but Zachary didn't want to find out if that was true.

He could hear a screech of static as one of the metallic stun balls sailed past his ear, barely missing his shoulder. He glanced back and could see that three trainees in yellow jerseys were gaining on him. One of them was an outerverse exchange whose primitive wings didn't allow full flight but made jumping over obstacles effortless. Zachary had taken Loren's advice to heart, but some of the older trainees had sniffed out his hiding spot on the warp-glove training course faster than he expected. Now he and his teammate were sprinting for the edge of the purple team's safety zone.

"Go!" Zachary's teammate called. "I can't keep up."

"We're almost there," Zachary shouted back.

But it didn't matter. A stun ball struck the trainee squarely in the back, tightening every muscle in his body and turning him into a breathing statue. Zachary's nostrils were invaded by a familiar scent: the smell of burning ozone after a lightning strike.

Zachary would surely be next. He braced himself even as he ran along the muddy ground, still wet from the storm. Then an arm stretched down from the treetops and grabbed him, pulling him fifteen feet upward. There was only one person at Indigo 8 capable of such a feat.

"Ryic," Zachary said, coming face-to-face with his bunkmate.

Ryic was perched in the tree alongside Kaylee. Both were wearing green jerseys over their shirts. Kaylee immediately launched a trio of stun balls down at Zachary's pursuers. As each of the balls made contact with its intended target, the three trainees in yellow were immobilized.

"Thanks," Zachary said.

"Don't thank us," Kaylee said. "We were using you as lizard bait. We've been trying to wipe out the yellow team's assassins for the last twenty minutes."

"You really know how to make a guy feel special, don't you?" Zachary replied.

Just then, a loud horn blared, signaling the end of the game. Cerebella's voice rang out over Indigo 8's PA system.

"Today's Chameleon game has been suspended. This evening's bonfire will be taking place early. Please remove your jerseys and proceed down to the lake."

Zachary, Ryic, and Kaylee all exchanged looks.

"How disappointing," Ryic said. "We do not get to enjoy competitive sport on Klenarog. We view it as a waste of time to do something whose outcome is so meaning-less. But now I see that my people are missing out."

Ryic lowered the others to the ground, then swung himself down as well. A pair of trainees wearing purple jerseys ran past them, heading back in the direction of the sleeping quarters.

"Hey, either of you know what happened?" Kaylee called.

"Stun ball malfunction," one of the trainees replied. "Set one of the green team's jerseys on fire."

"But apparently nobody got too badly hurt," the other added.

They continued on. Zachary, Kaylee, and Ryic walked through the woods toward the grassy slope between the lake and the Ulam.

"Well, consider yourself lucky," Kaylee said to Zachary.

"My next stun ball had your name on it."

"How do you know I wasn't going to get you first?" Zachary shot back.

"I've seen your aim on the starchery range. I wasn't worried."

"Can those frail little arms of yours even pull the string on a photon bow?" Zachary asked.

"I guess there's only one way to settle this," Kaylee said. "Another bet. We'll see whose aim is really better. Besides, I've gotten used to the way you fold my shirts."

"Oh, it's on," Zachary said.

The two took a turn away from the grassy slope and began heading uphill through the dense forest toward the starchery range.

"Um, guys," Ryic said. "That is not the way to the lake."

"Come on," Kaylee said. "We need an official scorekeeper."

"Wait. You're going to sneak onto the starchery range now? Without supervision? That's a clear violation of campus rules."

"If we cut through the woods, no one will even see us," Kaylee said.

"You're welcome to head to the bonfire without us," Zachary said. "We shouldn't be too long."

Ryic appeared conflicted.

"Well, I can't very well let you go without a lookout." Ryic shook his head. "What is this apparent mind control you're able to enact on me? Making me do things I normally wouldn't do?"

"It's called peer pressure," Kaylee said.

"Well, I don't like it," Ryic said.

After a short walk through the woods, they reached the empty starchery range, which sprawled out in the shadow of the Ulam. Ryic was twisting his head practically in circles to make sure nobody was around to see what they were doing. Zachary and Kaylee approached a long rack and each chose a photon bow—which looked like a regular bow, except the string was glowing. There was no need to put arrows in these bows. Merely pull and release and a beam of superheated light called a photon bolt would shoot forth.

"First person to tag three targets wins," Kaylee said matter-of-factly.

Zachary nodded.

They each lifted their weapon and prepared to fire. As Zachary's thumb and forefinger pulled back on the tightened string, he felt it warm up, a flicker of light forming at his fingertips.

"Ryic, first targets," Kaylee said.

Ryic pressed a button on a metal pedestal, and a hundred yards away a robotic arm sent two jet-propelled crystal cubes airborne. They began spiraling randomly through the sky.

Kaylee released her fingers from the string, and a beam of light shot out, sailing in a perfectly straight line for one of the targets. It looked as if it was going to score a direct hit, but the cube zigged at the last second, avoiding it.

The heat between Zachary's fingertips was almost too blistering to withstand. He took a moment longer before he let his photon bolt fly. His beam cruised toward the other target and, unlike Kaylee's, it made contact with the cube, blasting it into tiny electrified shards.

"That's one for me," Zachary said.

Ryic pressed the button again, and another pair of crystal cubes were launched into the sky. This time Zachary and Kaylee both successfully tagged their aerial targets, destroying them.

As the third round commenced, Zachary felt something slimy wiggle up his pants leg. It was cold, wet, and quickly tightening its grip on his skin. He swatted at the lump beneath his pants and a cool, fleshy mass slipped out and hit the ground. Zachary recognized it as one of the sluglike creatures from the Ulam hallway's wintery terrarium. Before he could hit at it again, it was slithering off.

"I didn't know vreeks existed on Earth," said Ryic. "I thought they were only native to the tundra planets."

"They are," Kaylee said.

Ryic's eyes went wide. "We need to stop it!"

As the creature made a beeline toward the lake, Zachary turned his photon bow and pulled the string.

"Not like that!" shouted Ryic.

But it was too late. The beam of light shot out and hit the vreek directly on its back. Instead of killing the creature, the shot split it in half and made two of them, each one growing larger than the first.

"Vreeks thrive on heat," Ryic explained. "Extreme temperatures actually multiply them."

They watched as the two creatures slimed their way out of sight.

"Where did it come from?" Kaylee asked.

"I don't know," Ryic said. "But if they make it to the bonfire, there are going to be a lot more of them."

Zachary and Kaylee dropped their bows, and the three sprinted back through the woods for the grassy hill that led down to the lake. Even with a killer space slug on the loose, Zachary couldn't shake the giddy feeling bubbling inside him. The camaraderie, the adventure, even the danger. It was everything he'd hoped Indigo 8 would be.

The bonfire had already begun when they arrived. Piles of wood and thin copper strips had been stacked at the center of a ring of rocks, and the fire's otherworldly green color gave everyone around it an emerald glow.

Most of the Starbounders-in-training were already sitting on stone benches, paper plates loaded with cookout food balanced on their knees. A trail of meat-scented smoke drifted from a row of industrial-sized gas grills. There was also a make-your-own-sundae table with an ice-cream freezer behind it.

Zachary, Kaylee, and Ryic had reached the outer circle of the bonfire. They looked around frantically but saw no sign of the vreeks anywhere. Zachary spotted Kwan sitting with the Lightwing boys.

"Kwan," he called as he hurried toward him.

"Hey, there you are. I've been looking for you."

"I was up at the starchery range," Zachary said between breaths. "Somehow one of those vreeks from the Ulam terrarium got—"

"Starchery range?" Kwan asked, cutting him off. "You know you're not allowed to be there without a trainer."

"Listen. There are vreeks coming this way. You have to do something."

Just then a trainee with the Indigo 8 infinity sign shaved into the hair on the side of his head pointed down at the ground.

"Loose vreek!" he yelled as he dived to try and grab it.

The creature easily slipped through his hands and propelled itself toward the bonfire. The other vreek was squirming its way past a group of third-year girls from the Cometeers SQ.

"Don't let them get to the fire," Ryic shouted.

°°–°– 🔂 –––°

Resident advisors and trainees tried to stop them, but the vreeks had already disappeared into the heart of the flames. A moment later, more than a dozen creatures emerged from the fire. The original vreek had been no bigger than a fist, but its mutated siblings each had grown to the size of an enormous crocodile. And there were no burns on their slimy bodies or any other signs of harm from the fire. Quite the opposite: the heat had turned the two slugs into a pack of vicious alien life-forms, stronger, faster, and much more aggressive than before.

Zachary watched as one of the new vreeks flung itself onto the back of a fleeing Lightwing girl. The force knocked her face-first into the dirt. The vreek was about to bite into the back of her neck when Monica kicked the supersized outerverse beast clear off her.

Resident advisors—including Kwan and Derek—were now wielding their warp gloves, using them to push slow-moving Starbounders-in-training out of the way of the onslaught of space slugs. Instructor Avendale and a few other trainers dashed out of a nearby equipment shed armed with what looked like high-tech fire extinguishers—metal hoses attached to handheld, frost-encrusted tanks. They sprayed blasts of freezing vapor at a pair of vreeks that were attacking the kitchen staff. Enveloped in the icy mists, the creatures let out high-pitched squeals and quickly slowed to a crawl. After another blast they were frozen solid.

Zachary turned to see a mucus-oozing vreek barrel past two of the trainers, knocking aside one of the stone benches as if it were made of balsa wood. Its gelatinous feelers seemed to be sampling the air, in hungry pursuit of human flesh. After a prolonged, deliberate sniff, the vreek honed in on Zachary. He wasn't sure if the creature was still angry from being shot with his photon bow, but it was heading straight for him and Kaylee with what definitely looked like vengeance on its primitive mind.

"I didn't shoot you," Kaylee said, pointing at Zachary. "He did!"

Ryic stretched his malleable arms to double their length. At first, Zachary thought Ryic was coming to their aid, but then he covered his own head and curled into a ball. His skin suddenly hardened into a rock-solid exoskeleton.

"Zachary, Kaylee, follow my lead," Ryic called out.

"Do I *look* like an armadillo?" Zachary asked.

Zachary made a running dive over the cookout table and slid up beside the ice-cream freezer. Kaylee followed behind him, taking cover nearby. Zachary could hear the still-charging vreek coming closer and he could feel his own heart beating faster. He took a breath and reminded himself that he was a Night and he was going to be okay.

Zachary pulled the cooling hose out from the back of the white tub and pointed its nozzle at the vreek. He sent a blast of freezing air at the monstrous slug, immobilizing it instantly.

More vreeks remained on the loose, and seeing their mutant siblings incapacitated only made them angrier. One was about to take out its rage on a group of Lightwing boys huddled together, when a hand encased in a warp glove emerged from a black hole in space and grabbed the creature by its tail. With a tug, the slug was pulled into the void, and Zachary watched as the vreek appeared thirty feet away in Derek's grasp. He attempted to wrestle the thrashing beast to the ground, but the vreek managed to get its mouth around Derek's other hand and bite down hard. Derek let out a scream, and with good reason.

Zachary could see that three of his fingers had been swallowed up in the slug's maw. But before the vreek could eat more, an older female trainee armed with one of the extinguishers sent a blast of cold at the creature, freezing it in place.

The last of the vreeks were surrounded by a circle of trainees and resident advisors. Zachary couldn't see what was happening from where he stood beside the ice-cream freezer, but he let out a deep breath when the shrieking sounds echoing through the air finally stopped. The creatures had been subdued.

"We only have a few minutes before they thaw," Instructor Avendale said. "Let's hurry and get them down to the cargo dock. We'll load them into the subzero freezer. Whoever's responsible for this is going to be taking a one-way trip to an asteroid prison."

Zachary could see that she was glaring at Professor Olari.

"You should try some," Kaylee said.

Zachary turned to see that she was holding a bowl of ice cream topped with chocolate sauce and whipped cream.

"Really?" he asked. "During all of that, you decided to make a hot fudge sundae?"

"Well, I wasn't going to let perfectly good ice cream go to waste."

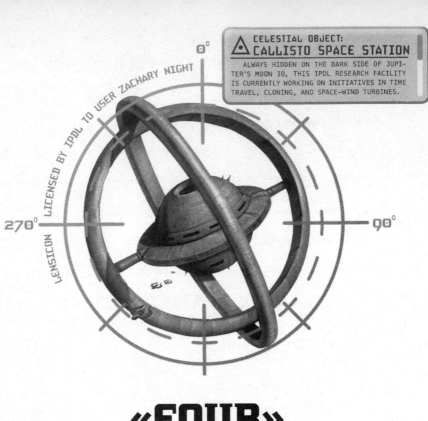

0°

270°

90°

LENSICON

⚠ CELESTIAL OBJECT:
△ CALLISTO SPACE STATION

ALWAYS HIDDEN ON THE DARK SIDE OF JUPI-
TER'S MOON IO, THIS IPDL RESEARCH FACILITY
IS CURRENTLY WORKING ON INITIATIVES IN TIME
TRAVEL, CLONING, AND SPACE-WIND TURBINES.

«FOUR»

Instructor Taylor, Indigo 8's galactic-safari guide, was standing at the front of the Ulam's briefing room. Her audience: thirty Lightwing boys and girls. They were being given one final lesson before departing on their first adventure into the outerverse. Zachary could hardly sleep the night before, and it wasn't because of all the excitement at the bonfire. He, like every other kid in his SQ, had huge hopes and expectations about this trip.

Instructor Taylor was showing them how to insert a lensicon, a contact lens with instant image recognition, allowing its user to identify whatever she or he was looking at.

"Gently rest the lens on your fingertip before placing it in your eye," she said with a slight Southern drawl.

Instructor Taylor was joined by two others who'd accompany the Starbounders-in-training into space: Professor Olari, who would be identifying all the wondrous creatures that passed by outside the ship's viewing pods; and Dr. Carlos Rodrijo, a renowned celestial physicist who would be explaining the principles of spaceflight and galactic folds.

Zachary pried his lower eyelid open and slid his lensicon over his right eye. Immediately his vision became blurry and he thought maybe he had inserted it incorrectly. He was about to remove it when suddenly his vision cleared and a tiny set of crosshairs appeared in his sightline. Zachary reached out to touch it, but of course it wasn't there; it was a projection created by the lensicon.

"Each lens has been programmed with an encyclopedic database of every living and nonliving thing that has been discovered in the universe," Instructor Taylor said. "To activate it, target an object within the crosshairs and blink twice."

Zachary's eyes scanned the room, and the first object he focused on was a clear mouthpiece resting on a table behind Instructor Taylor. It looked similar to one that would be used for scuba diving, except it wasn't connected to any tanks. He oriented the tiny crosshairs so they targeted the mouthpiece, and blinked twice. As soon as he did, words appeared to float in midair; a heads-up display of information scrolled beside the mouthpiece.

> ⚠ TERRESTRIAL OBJECT:
> **OFF-PLANET BIO REGULATOR**
>
> THIS DEVICE, CREATED FOR OXYGEN-BREATHING LIFE-FORMS, PRODUCES A SUSTAINABLE ENVIRONMENT WHEN INSERTED INTO A SPECIES' O_2 INTAKE HOLE.
>
> IN ADDITION, IT GENERATES A THIN MAGNETIC REPULSIVE BARRIER AROUND THE USER'S BODY TO PROTECT IT FROM PARTICLE DEBRIS IN THE VACUUM OF SPACE.

A table of contents listing various subheadings followed, including **HISTORY**, **STRUCTURE AND FUNCTION**, **PERFORMANCE**, and **COMPLICATIONS**. Zachary turned his head before reading any further. This time his eyes fell on Professor Olari. He blinked twice.

LIFE-FORM: CLIPSIAN

THIS SPECIES HAILS FROM THE RINGED PLANETS OF TARTAROC.

FUELED BY PHYSIOLOGICAL INTERNAL COMBUSTION, THEIR ENERGY COMES FROM A SUPERHEATED CORE THAT SUSTAINS THEM FOR APPROXIMATELY ONE HUNDRED YEARS WITH NO NEED FOR FOOD, LIGHT, OR CHEMICAL INTAKE. THUS THEY ARE CAPABLE OF SURVIVING IN THE HARSHEST OF CONDITIONS.

WHILE MOST HAVE BECOME PHILOSOPHERS AND THINKERS, THE MORE AGGRESSIVE WAR TRIBES, UNDER THE COMMAND OF GENERAL NIBIRU, HAVE RAVAGED HUNDREDS OF DEFENSELESS POPULATED PLANETS.

Zachary was about to skip down to a menu subheading titled **CONFLICT WITH THE IPDL** when he felt a hand on his shoulder. He turned to see an imposing man with especially dark eyebrows standing behind him. Ryic and Kaylee were at his side.

"Mr. Night, come with me," the man said. He directed his gaze to Kylee and Ryic. "Director Madsen would like to have a word with the three of you."

Zachary's chest tightened. He stood up and joined his friends, and the man ushered them from the briefing room. The other Lightwings were too preoccupied with their lensicons to even notice.

Zachary, Kaylee, and Ryic kept silent on the walk to Director Madsen's office. Zachary knew they'd broken the rules by sneaking onto the starchery range, and he feared that some punishment was now coming. He tried to look relaxed, but his shoulders still felt like they were rising up to his ears.

The man with the eyebrows led them through a series of sloping corridors before arriving at a metal door. It opened, and a figure emerged, his face partially covered by a mask and his arms cloaked in long sleeves and gloves. It was impossible to tell if he was human or not. He passed the group without acknowledging them, and even the man with the eyebrows stepped out of his way.

The metal door had looked identical to any other, but Zachary was surprised by the room they found inside. The walls had been covered with wood paneling that made it look like the captain's quarters of an old-fashioned pirate ship. Sitting behind a large oak desk was an older black man with a curly gray goatee. He wore a fleece vest over a white T-shirt and a baseball cap with the Indigo 8 insignia—an infinity symbol with two ringed planets orbiting around it—on the front. A black Labrador lay on the floor beside him.

"Please," Director Madsen said, gesturing to the chairs opposite his desk. "Let's talk about what happened last night. We're lucky no one was severely hurt. Even Derek escaped just needing a few artificial fingers."

Zachary, Kaylee, and Ryic sat down. Zachary had the same queasy feeling he got the time he was called to the principal's office after a hallway scuffle with a bully.

"I know you were on the starchery range around the same time those vreeks got loose. Did you see anything suspicious? We know those creatures escaped from the Ulam. Notice anyone in the vicinity of the building?"

Zachary leaned forward in the hard wooden seat. His

fingers nervously played with the deactivated warp glove in his pocket. He cleared his throat before speaking up.

"No. I felt something on the back of my leg and when I looked down, it was a vreek."

"We tried to warn Kwan at the bonfire, but it was too late," Kaylee added.

"For that, I applaud you," Madsen said.

Zachary exchanged looks with Ryic and Kaylee. Suddenly all that tension that had built up in his shoulders released. His worry was gone.

"But you broke the rules by trespassing on the starchery range," Madsen said, eyeing each of them in turn. "Your actions need to be punished. For your misconduct, you all just got yourself custodial duty. You'll be serving under Captain Wilcox on one of the freight ships heading out today."

"Today?" Zachary asked, now feeling angry. "But we leave for our galactic safari in an hour."

"Unfortunately you won't be going on that trip," Madsen said. "You'll still get your first spaceflight. Only instead of stargazing and celestial sightseeing, you'll be mopping up lunar mold."

Zachary's body was twisting inside. He remembered his parents and brother telling him how their first galactic safaris were the most magical experience of their lives. He wanted to snap back with another argument, but he knew it would only make things worse.

"Look on the bright side. I could have set your punishment on Saturday during the Octocentennial celebration."

All of Indigo 8 had been buzzing about this. On Friday, every IPDL officer within 500 million light years would be gathered at Indigo 8 for the feast and ceremony. Except for the Elite Corps Starbounders, like Jacob, whose covert mission would never allow them to leave their posts.

"Please," Zachary said. "This isn't fair. I'll miss the Octocentennial. I'll do chores around campus for the rest of the year. Anything to go on that trip."

"I'm sorry, son," Madsen said. "My decision is final. Mr. DiSalvo will take you all down to the freighter. That will be all."

The man with the eyebrows stood waiting by the door as Zachary got up from his chair and started to leave. Ryic and Kaylee followed, equally disappointed. Then Zachary stopped and turned back to Madsen.

"Look, this was my idea," he said. "Don't make Ryic and Kaylee lose out, too."

"You're all accountable for your actions," Madsen said. "So you'll all be punished equally."

Zachary walked out the door with Ryic and Kaylee behind him.

Instead of taking them back to the briefing room, DiSalvo led them down a side tunnel.

"Zachary, thanks for trying to cover for us," Kaylee said.

"This sucks," he replied.

DiSalvo ushered the trio onto a large open platform that shot down hundreds of feet into the bowels of the Ulam. Zachary could feel wind blowing up through his hair and see flashes of each descending floor as they sped down. They passed the infirmary on one, flight simulators hanging from the ceilings on another, and a room the size of a hockey rink filled with nothing but computer mainframes and circuit boards.

"That's as close as you'll ever get to Cerebella," DiSalvo said, referring to the maze of processors and hard drives.

Zachary knew that Cerebella pretty much ran Indigo 8, controlling everything from the voice-activated pathways to the gravity modulator in the Qube to the launch portals in the starship hangar. But it hadn't occurred to him that she was operating from somewhere inside the grounds. She just seemed to exist.

The platform passed a few more floors before coming to a soft stop. DiSalvo and the three trainees walked through an archway that marked the entrance to an enormous underground space hangar. Whatever anger and frustration Zachary felt after leaving Madsen's office disappeared when he got his first up-close look at all of the starships docked underground. He didn't know where to turn first.

"Check those out," Kaylee said. "Pitchforks."

She was pointing at a row of silver fighter ships shaped like tridents, the ancient three-pronged spears that Poseidon famously wielded. Each ship had a cockpit on top and an upside-down cockpit on the bottom. Zachary blinked twice, and his lensicon began scrolling text, but he was too busy staring at the ships to read about them.

"Looks a little strange, doesn't it?" DiSalvo asked.

"But in space there is no top or bottom. And you can be attacked from all sides."

Just the thought of twirling in space sent a new rush of endorphins pumping through Zachary. As they moved deeper into the hangar, Zachary spied Instructor Taylor, Professor Olari, Dr. Rodrijo, and all the Lightwing boys and girls boarding a spectacular ship shaped like a corkscrew with dozens of clear glass pods, one for each passenger, affixed to the outside.

"That's a clairvoyant," DiSalvo said, pointing to the ship. "It rotates on its axis as it travels through space, making sure its passengers never miss a thing from inside their viewing pods."

Seeing the ship was like rubbing salt in the wound for Zachary. What would his family say when they found out he'd gotten freighter duty after just one week at Indigo 8? Jacob would never let him hear the end of it.

DiSalvo directed them toward the far side of the cavernous room, where a pair of lighted underground runways stretched for what seemed like miles into the darkness. They passed a row of golden ships that were shaped like enormous double-headed battle-axes. These were the pride of the fleet—the top of the line for combat. Workers were busy using rotating diamond wheels to sharpen the blades protruding from the ships' sides.

Up ahead, Zachary spotted long robotic arms lifting a massive subzero freezer toward the back of a rectangular space freighter. Its name, *Dreadnought Epsilon*, was hard to read under the grime and dings from asteroid hits. Crew members were directing aux-bots to badly damaged spots on the ship's hull for quick repairs before takeoff.

DiSalvo came to a stop. "This is the dreadnought you'll be serving your disciplinary duties on," he said.

"I've seen garbage trucks that look like they could fly better than that," Kaylee said.

A ramp descended from the side of the spacecraft, and a man who looked about Zachary's dad's age walked up to them. He had tattoos on the backs of his hands and neck. They'd been inked on with neon dyes that gave his skin a colorful glow. His jacket seemed to be made from the leathery skin of some alien beast.

"So, are these my mop monkeys?" he asked.

"Star-bound and ready, Captain Wilcox," DiSalvo replied.

"Good, 'cause we had a sewage valve burst during our last jump. Whole cabin is covered in lunar mold. There are buckets and mag mops waiting inside."

The robotic arms were creaking above them as they tried to get the large subzero freezer into the cargo hold. But instead of making a clean entry, the freezer slammed into the ship's outer wall. Zachary could hear the muffled wailing of the captive vreeks inside the freezer.

"Easy there," Wilcox shouted to the crew member who was manipulating the arms from a nearby control panel. "Let's try to keep that freezer secure. I don't need those vreeks breaking out midflight."

Zachary, Ryic, and Kaylee continued to stand there.

"What are you waiting for?" Wilcox snapped. "I'm not rolling out a red carpet."

DiSalvo stayed behind on the hangar floor as they boarded the dreadnought. A crew member handed them custodial jumpsuits to put over their cargo pants and Indigo 8 T-shirts. Zachary had been expecting some kind of special spacesuit, but apparently this was all he was going to get.

Zachary and his friends were standing in a cabin about

the size of a three-car garage. There were thin window slits along the sides and a flight deck up front. The massive cargo hold where the vreeks were stored was in the back by the engines. Two additional crew members were already on board making final preparations for departure. One was securing all the open compartments, while the other strapped maintenance tools inside the underbins.

The crew member who had handed them their jumpsuits pointed them over to three metal buckets, each with what looked like an old-fashioned string mop propped up inside. They were just wondering what exactly to do with them when Wilcox thundered back into the cabin.

"You'll have to save the cleaning for later," he bellowed. "The galactic fold outside Saturn is shifting. We've got to leave now or we'll never make it to the tundra planet on schedule."

Wilcox started for the cockpit. Five other crew members—the ones who had been directing the aux-bots and controlling the robotic arms—boarded the dreadnought, joining the others already inside.

"Everybody harness up," Wilcox called, strapping himself into the pilot's seat in the flight deck.

Zachary looked around and saw the crew members insert themselves into the mechanical webbing on the walls, slipping their arms and legs through the mesh before it automatically tightened, securing them in place. Kaylee harnessed herself in easily, but Ryic was struggling. To Zachary, it felt a lot like getting tangled up in a hammock. As the mesh tightened, Zachary had to wonder how safe he'd really be in an emergency.

Through the open flight-deck door he could see Wilcox slip off his jacket, flex his fingers, and begin to activate the ship's holographic display. The dreadnought's entryway closed like the shutter of a digital camera.

It's really happening, Zachary thought as the faint hum of an engine and the dimming rows of interior lights signaled that they were getting closer to takeoff. Through his window slit Zachary could see that the ground engineers outside were wincing from the noise despite their large protective headgear.

"You've done this before, right?" Zachary asked Ryic. "I mean, you had to get to Earth from Klenarog somehow."

"Oh, yes. I took a shuttle to the main IPDL hub near the Xero System. Then the other outerverse exchanges and I were brought to Indigo 8 on a freighter not much different from this one."

"What was it like?"

"Delightful," Ryic said. "Although I did regurgitate my second stomach during takeoff."

Zachary tried to move as far away from Ryic as possible, but with the webbing holding him fast, he could only shift a few inches.

He peered back into the flight deck to watch Wilcox controlling the ship, guiding his hands through the air before him like Zachary's old music teacher conducting the school orchestra.

Zachary felt the ship lift off and he looked out his window. They were ten feet up above the ground. The dreadnought lumbered forward before it started picking up speed, passing runway lights that created a strobe effect, giving Zachary the feeling that he was moving in slow motion.

"Cerebella, initiate the launch portal," Wilcox said.

Through the flight-deck window at the front of the ship, Zachary could see they were speeding for a steel wall, and at ever-increasing velocity. A head-on collision seemed imminent. Zachary wanted to call a warning to Wilcox, but it was all happening so fast he couldn't get the words out. He was bracing himself for impact when a black disc formed, just like the ones Starbounders reached their warp gloves through, only much, much bigger. The dreadnought flew straight into it.

For a second, it seemed to Zachary as if gravity was pulling him in every direction, like it wanted to tear him apart. He knew he was neither on Earth nor in space, but inside the galactic fold between them. He had been told that the laws of physics stopped taking effect in this place. His body felt like every molecule and atom was suddenly shifting. Unless his vision was playing tricks on him, the ship and his body were rippling like waves in the ocean. But as quickly as all these strange sensations had arrived, they disappeared. Suddenly, Zachary was weightless. They were in space.

The protective webbing released, allowing him to work his way out of it and float freely through the cabin. Kaylee drifted up beside him. "Hey," Ryic called. "I'm stuck." He wriggled and squirmed to get loose, and Kaylee went to help him, but Zachary's attention was caught by the outside view.

The ship had emerged in the orbit of Jupiter. His lensicon informed him that they were between Io and Europa, Jupiter's two largest moons.

Zachary peered into the blackness. He could see dozens of other moons of Jupiter hanging in space like part of a mobile with no strings. Then in the shadow of Io he spied a massive gyroscopic space station, with two giant concentric rings each spinning on independent axes. The superstructure floated in space, surrounded by a squadron of pitchforks that seemed to protect it. Zachary focused his lensicon and blinked twice.

⚠ CELESTIAL OBJECT:
CALLISTO SPACE STATION

ALWAYS HIDDEN ON THE DARK SIDE OF JUPITER'S MOON IO, THIS IPDL RESEARCH FACILITY IS CURRENTLY WORKING ON INITIATIVES IN TIME TRAVEL, CLONING, AND SPACE-WIND TURBINES.

POWERED BY ONE OF ONLY THREE KNOWN PERPETUAL ENERGY GENERATORS, IT SERVES AS A COMMUNICATIONS RELAY FOR IPDL TRANSMISSIONS

AND HANDLES ALL DATA STORAGE AND PROCESSING FOR INDIGO 8'S MAINFRAME COMPUTER, CEREBELLA.

ITS CONCENTRIC SPINNING RINGS SIMULATE EARTH'S GRAVITY TO PERFECT EFFECT, CREATING A NONHAZARDOUS WORK ENVIRONMENT INSIDE.

The *Dreadnought Epsilon* blasted past the station, dipping toward Saturn, where Wilcox had said the next fold was located. Hovering by the cabin door, Zachary, Ryic, and Kaylee each stared silently out through the captain's windows. It might not have been a galactic safari, but it was still space. And about a billion times more exciting than life in Kingston.

"Okay, monkeys," Captain Wilcox called from the flight deck. "You're not here to be looky-loos. Time to get to work. And I need one of you up here."

Ryic and Kaylee both turned to Zachary, none too eager.

"Go ahead," Ryic said.

"How generous of you," Zachary replied.

"Actually I was being selfish," Ryic said. "I have no desire to spend time with Wilcox. In fact, I'm quite intimidated by him."

Zachary floated to the flight deck and maneuvered himself inside.

"These mold spores have even found their way into the underbins," Wilcox said. "There are rags in the box over there."

Zachary pulled open a drawer in the box and retrieved the cleaning supplies. He began wiping down the surface of the storage cases beneath the flight-deck chairs. As he worked, his eyes wandered to the endless expanse that sprawled out before him through the front window. Zachary's attention moved to the ship's holographic display, which was projecting an elaborate diagram on the glass. It appeared to be a detailed rendering of the outerverse with colored tubes connecting distant points, not unlike the subway maps he'd seen on a school field trip to DC. A ship icon was heading toward one of the tube entrances. Was it theirs?

"Those walls aren't going to clean themselves," Wilcox snapped. Zachary turned from the display. "What, you've never seen a Kepler cartograph before?"

Zachary shook his head.

"You can't just bound anywhere you want, anytime you want. You have to use the folds in space that are already there. Without the cartograph we'd be lost in the outerverse."

Zachary knew from his flight-simulation activity at Indigo 8 and his training at home that every spacecraft had an internal navigation system called a starbox, containing maps and an autopilot. It was the heart and brain of any ship. Of course, he had never seen one in action before.

Zachary resumed scrubbing the underbins and caught a glimpse through the open flight-deck door of Kaylee and Ryic using the mops to clean up the cabin's floors and ceiling. The stringy mopheads were magnetically clinging to whatever surface they made contact with, soaking up all the mold they touched. Zachary finished wiping down two of the underbins before Wilcox ordered him to his harness.

Zachary pushed off, floating back to where Ryic and Kaylee were already strapping themselves in. It wasn't long before Zachary could see sharp prongs emerge from the front of the dreadnought. They began to pulse, and suddenly another interdimensional fold opened. The dread-nought shot through the hole, Zachary once again felt as if he was spinning like a top.

When the ship emerged, the sun that he knew was gone and the celestial atmosphere had a blue-green glow that reminded him of the bonfire where the vreeks had multiplied back at Indigo 8.

"We just arrived at the outer ring of the Milky Way," Wilcox announced. "Approximately ninety thousand light years from Earth. The next bound will take us to the edge of the Stringer Nebula. Sit tight. It won't be long."

He wasn't kidding. Barely a minute passed before the dreadnought was jumping through another fold. This time the ship exited into a solar system that had two suns and hundreds of planets orbiting them.

"Just one more leap to the tundra planet," Wilcox said. "Crew, grab your spaste pouches and eat up. Mop monkeys, you'll dine when this ship is sparkling like an aux-bot's rear end."

Once again the webbing released, and Zachary and Kaylee were free. And once again, Ryic remained stuck in the harness.

"Clearly these were not built for Klenarogians," he said philosophically.

Zachary and Kaylee floated over to help, but before they could pull Ryic loose, a loud crash sounded from the cargo hold. One of the crew members gave an exasperated sigh.

"The vreeks are getting restless," he said. "I'll go lower the freezer's temperature. See if a little more cold won't calm them down."

He soared through the cabin to the cargo hold entrance and disappeared inside.

"Get a move on, ragboy," Wilcox shouted at Zachary.

"I think he likes you," Kaylee said.

Just then, a blast echoed from the back of the dreadnought. The crew member who'd gone to check on the vreeks spiraled out of the cargo hold with a hole seared straight through his Indigo 8 jumpsuit. He hit the wall and reached out, grabbing Zachary's leg.

"The ship is being hijacked," he said with his last breath.

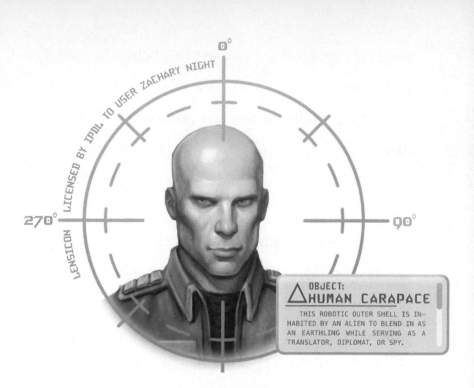

0°

270°

90°

OBJECT:
△ HUMAN CARAPACE

THIS ROBOTIC OUTER SHELL IS IN-
HABITED BY AN ALIEN TO BLEND IN AS
AN EARTHLING WHILE SERVING AS A
TRANSLATOR, DIPLOMAT, OR SPY.

«FIVE»

"You three! Up here!" Wilcox commanded Zachary, Ryic, and Kaylee.

The remaining crew members were grabbing sonic crossbows from the underbins, and Zachary and Kaylee were tugging at the webbing still holding Ryic captive.

"Come on, Ryic," Kaylee said.

"I'm trying!" he cried, struggling to pull himself free.

Zachary wasn't sure what was about to come out

from the rear hold, but he certainly didn't want to wait to find out.

"Lock down the cargo area!" Wilcox shouted back to the cabin.

A crew member raced over to try to close the door, but a lightning ball struck him in the chest and sent him tumbling backward through the air.

Six alien figures emerged from the open cargo hold. But these weren't the vreeks. They were a grizzly-looking crew of off-planet thugs, armed with voltage slingshots and sonic crossbows. Zachary noticed that they all had shockles on their wrists and ankles, but the chains of pure electricity that connected them had been deactivated.

"Go without me!" Ryic shouted to Zachary and Kaylee. "I'm still stuck."

Zachary hurried to one of the cabin's underbins and unstrapped a pocketknife from the row of maintenance tools. He raced back to slash through the webbing still binding Ryic. Two of the nearby hijackers—emaciated creatures of fur and bone—snarled like wolves. They charged at the crew member closest to the cargo hold, tackling him to the ceiling.

"Mayday, Mayday!" Zachary could hear Wilcox calling urgently from the flight deck. "This is *Dreadnought Epsilon*. We have hostiles on the ship. Current location is two hundred and forty thousand miles outside Space Fold DES-762. Coordinates X-120, Y-26, Z-201. Immediate assistance requested."

The dreadnought's crew members sent concentrated beams of sound flying from their sonic crossbows. An all-out battle for control of the ship was under way. Zachary, Ryic, and Kaylee pushed themselves off and headed for the relative safety of the flight deck. Zachary looked over his shoulder as a beam of sound hit one of the hijackers, which had more in common with an amoeba than any mammal or human. The creature burst like a popped tomato.

"Let's move!" Wilcox shouted. "Three Lightwings dying on my watch is not my idea of how to get a promotion."

They made one final lunge, gliding safely inside the flight deck. Wilcox punched a button on the wall, and the cockpit door sealed shut.

The sounds of the battle continued in the cabin. The door did little to mute the explosions and screams on the other side.

"How long until Indigo 8 sends help?" Zachary asked.

"Indigo 8?" Wilcox repeated. "That signal won't reach Earth. Best we can hope for is somebody from the nearby prospecting station hearing it and coming this way."

A loud blast struck the flight-deck door, causing it to bend in.

"Put your warp gloves on," Wilcox ordered Zachary, Ryic, and Kaylee.

Zachary had almost forgotten about the metal orb sitting in his pocket. He reached in and removed the sphere, holding it in the palm of his hand. He squeezed his thumb and pinkie together, and with a whir the gauntlet extended down his arm.

Ryic and Kaylee gloved up as well.

Warning lights began to flash on the cockpit window.

"Something's wrong! The starbox must have shorted," Wilcox said.

A thundering boom rocked the flight-deck door, this time blowing it open. One of the six hijackers, a muscular, olive-skinned beast, stood there with photon cannons under two of his four arms. These shotgun-sized weapons could fire double blasts of superheated light that could turn steel into Swiss cheese. The creature gave a slobbering laugh, drool dripping down its thorny chin.

To Zachary's astonishment, Wilcox said, "We surrender. The ship is yours."

He lifted his hands above his head. But not to surrender. In one fluid motion, he grabbed a voltage slingshot from a hidden compartment on the ceiling and fired at the hijacker. The electrically charged ammunition struck the creature square in the chest, shocking it with such force that the beast went spiraling backward.

The surviving crew members in the cabin were doing their best to keep the remaining hijackers from reaching the flight deck. Wilcox turned to the holographic display on the front window. The emergency backup lights were blinking, including a prompt that read, MIE WITH PELE ϙ IMMINENT.

"What's an MIE?" Ryic asked.

"Major impact event," Wilcox answered. "We're going to crash into that planet if we can't adjust course."

In the distance, Zachary saw a red-tinted planet. It was getting bigger by the second. Wilcox's fingers were moving furiously in the air.

"The starbox isn't responding at all," he said. "If I'm not able to override it—"

But he didn't get to finish. A photon bolt hit him in the back of the neck, knocking him out cold. Zachary spun around and looked into the cabin. Only two IPDL guards were still conscious, and the pair of emaciated wolflike creatures stood menacingly over them.

"Try not to eat them, Jahir," said a hijacker that looked human, even though his skin was a little grayer and his biceps were bigger than any Zachary had ever seen. "We might need them as hostages later."

Jahir gnashed his teeth. "But Skold, I'm hungry."

Skold ignored him and headed toward the flight deck. Zachary, Ryic, and Kaylee hadn't budged since Wilcox had been struck down. As Skold approached, Zachary noticed that his eyes moved strangely, shifting unnaturally and rarely blinking.

"We've got three kids in the flight deck," Skold called back to his fellow hijackers. "Kur'tuo, get up here and watch them."

Skold didn't even look at the young Starbounders-in-training. He clearly didn't consider them a threat. His attention was on the blaring warnings on the window.

Zachary still held the pocketknife in his ungloved hand. He knew that if he was going to defend himself and his friends, he'd have to do it now. He thrust the blade right for Skold's rib cage, but in the same instant, the alien grabbed Zachary's wrist and twisted, causing the knife to drop from his hand. Skold whipped his head around and glared at Zachary.

"Don't try to be the hero," he said. "It never ends well."

Kur'tuo, a creature that looked like a ten-foot-tall praying mantis, squeezed through the open flight-deck door. He stopped between Skold and Zachary, lifting his powerful arm up against Zachary's throat. Zachary could feel the serrated blades along the underside of the creature's arm cut into his chin.

Skold began waving his hands across the flight-deck window, trying to reactivate the starbox.

"It's not responding," he said.

Kur'tuo began making clicking noises with his mandibles.

"Don't you think I tried that?" Skold snapped back.

The warning on the window now read, `MIE COUNT-DOWN, 00:04:00.`

There were less than four minutes until impact, and the seconds kept ticking away. Zachary could now see the red-tinted surface of the planet clearly.

"Is that lava?" he asked.

"Lava is the expulsion from a volcano," Ryic replied. "When an entire planet is composed of the molten rock, it is called magma."

"Either way, we get melted like a stick of butter," Skold said.

Zachary couldn't help but think that, for an alien, Skold acted awfully human. The way he looked. The way he talked. Zachary watched as Skold jabbed his pocket-knife into the metal equipment panel and pried it open. In all the chaos, Zachary hadn't thought to use his lens-icon. Until now. He centered the crosshairs on Skold and blinked twice, expecting to read `LIFE-FORM`, but instead he read:

THIS ROBOTIC OUTER SHELL IS INHABITED BY
AN ALIEN TO BLEND IN AS AN EARTHLING WHILE
SERVING AS A TRANSLATOR, DIPLOMAT, OR SPY.

PRESENT INTERIOR LIFE-FORM: UNKNOWN.

Skold was some kind of robot with an alien living inside him?

Zachary turned back to the warning and saw that the MIE countdown had reached two minutes. The planet was way too close to the window. And Skold was head deep in the machinery of the ship.

"The IPDL is making it harder to hot-wire these things," he said. "All it used to take was a pair of pliers."

Skold reached for the voltage slingshot resting in Wilcox's limp hand and aimed it at the inside of the dreadnought's equipment panel.

"Are you crazy?" Kaylee asked. "You're going to kill us all!"

"We're already dead," Skold replied.

He fired off a blast, frying the panel. The cartograph

disappeared, along with all the other readings on the flight-deck window. But Skold's plan worked, because the ship shifted directions, its engines pushing it out of the gravitational pull of Pele 9.

"You did it!" Ryic said. "We aren't going to crash."

"Not into that planet," Skold said. "But I can't make any guarantees about that one." He pointed to a dusty, yellow-tinged planet with storm clouds moving across its surface.

Apparently, the electric surge had rebooted the starbox.

The flight-deck window became functional again, showing a warning that read, MIE WITH SIROCCO IMMINENT. MIE COUNTDOWN, 00:01:05.

"Everybody, brace for impact," Skold shouted.

The dreadnought rocketed into the highest band of Sirocco's atmosphere, juddering the interior like a wooden roller coaster.

"Come close," Ryic said to Zachary and Kaylee.

They gathered beside him and he stretched out his arms and torso to create a protective barrier around them. The last thing Zachary could see before Ryic covered his view completely was the ship plunging into a golden cloud. Zachary's teeth were shaking so violently that he feared they'd rattle right out of his head. His face was just inches away from Kaylee's. He could hear her heavy breath in his ear and then felt her fingers wrap around his, clutching them tightly.

"Don't worry," Zachary tried to reassure her. "We're going to be okay."

Suddenly the turbulence went away and the sensation of gravity returned. Everything was quiet for a moment, as if maybe they had made it out unscathed. And then came the impact.

Zachary and Kaylee, still within Ryic's protective shell, were thrown forward, slamming hard into something. The force of the collision broke Ryic's hold. Zachary's arm was stabbed by the sharpened edge of a broken object as he tumbled to the ground. Opening his eyes to get his bearings, he saw a crimson stain soaking through the sleeve of his jumpsuit. The sight of his own blood immediately sent a flush of pain shooting through his arm.

The entire flight-deck window was buried in the sand. Ryic and Kaylee were on the floor nearby, seemingly unhurt. Kur'tuo was clinging to the wall, having dug his arm blades into the metal surface.

Skold was lying on the ground, with a piece of the metal equipment panel piercing his side like a spear. Zachary rose to his knees and was about to stand when Kur'tuo dropped from the wall and stepped between Zachary and Skold. He gave Zachary a look as if to remind him how easy he would be to kill if he decided to get bold.

Skold pulled the shard of debris from his body, leaving a large hole that went straight into his center. Still kneeling, Zachary could see plastic and metal beyond the layer of phony flesh. And beyond that, inside a glass case, was something living. All Zachary could make out was a webbed foot and a tail. The crosshairs of his lensicon zeroed in on the creature, but before he could blink twice, Skold grabbed the jacket off Wilcox's chair and slipped it on, covering the hole.

"You three," he said to Zachary, Kaylee, and Ryic. "Up."

They slowly got to their feet. Zachary immediately felt off-balance. He realized that the ship was nearly vertical. The only way to get out of the flight deck was to climb *up* into the main cabin. Skold reached into the equipment panel he had pried open and removed an object that was roughly the size of a box of playing cards. It was solid indigo and had an infinity symbol on it. He pocketed the device and led the way, with Zachary, Ryic, and Kaylee behind him. Kur'tuo brought up the rear.

The dreadnought's main cabin was a grim scene. Those who hadn't been injured in the space battle had clearly suffered in the crash. The only beings still conscious were Jahir and his twin.

"This one's still breathing." Jahir pointed to an IPDL guard lying on the ground.

Suddenly the ship jolted downward. It was sinking into the sand. Skold punched a button to activate the departure ramp. But nothing happened.

"What good is an emergency exit door if it doesn't open during emergencies?" Skold demanded of no one in particular.

He picked up one of the discarded photon cannons and fired at the exit door. The blasts made slow progress, and it felt like the dreadnought was submerging faster.

"Jahir, Lalique, arm yourselves," Skold ordered. "We need more firepower."

The two emaciated wolven beasts took up sonic cross-bows and started firing at the same spot that Skold was blasting. Zachary bent down and reached for a weapon of his own. As his hand gripped one of the crossbows, Kur'tuo moved an arm blade inches away from his throat.

Zachary tried his best not to flinch, to keep his voice steady in the face of having his windpipe sliced open. "He said we needed more firepower."

Kur'tuo looked to Skold, who nodded to let Zachary join the attack. Finally, their combined firepower punc-tured a hole in the steel door, but the ship had already sunk so deep that sand started pouring inside. Quickly.

Kur'tuo scurried over and used his arms to saw away at the opening. The alien mantis started to turn the small hole into a larger one. Then, with a couple swift slashes of his blades, the gap became big enough to squeeze through.

"Go, go," Skold commanded.

Weapons still in hand, Kur'tuo, Jahir, and Lalique climbed for the planet's surface as sand flooded past them. Skold pushed Kaylee out through the hole, using his strength to propel her forward despite the tidal wave of sand crashing in. Ryic was next, and there was no time to waste. The ship's flight deck was filling up like the bottom of an hourglass.

Zachary turned back to the unconscious guard, whose body was halfway submerged in sand.

"What about him?" he asked.

"Remember what I told you about trying to be the hero," Skold replied.

"We can still get him out of here," Zachary said.

Zachary dropped the sonic crossbow and moved to the guard's side. He tried to shake him awake, but the IPDL officer felt cold and lifeless. Zachary put two fingers on his throat and couldn't find a pulse. Still not ready to give up, Zachary tried to lift the guard from the sand, but Skold grabbed Zachary by the back of his shirt, heaving him up over his shoulder.

"I need you alive," he said.

The alien hijacker scooped up a supply canister and vaulted himself out through the hole with Zachary in tow. As Skold swam against the current of sand, the fine particles washed over Zachary, invading his ears, his nose, and his tightly shut eyes. It felt like a thousand tiny daggers were scratching at Zachary's corneas. He had to squeeze his lips tightly to keep his mouth from filling up, too. Even so, stray grains slipped through, grinding between his teeth. Then Skold pulled himself to the surface. He put Zachary down, and they both hurried to solid footing.

Kur'tuo, Jahir, and Lalique stood together, watching with perverse delight as the dreadnought disappeared into the ground. More precisely, only the front half of it disappeared. Zachary hadn't realized that the back end of the space freighter had broken off during the crash and was a quarter of a mile away. Between the back end and the now-sunken nose of the ship were the remnants of the cargo hold. Rubberized crates and the subzero freezer littered the sandy landscape.

"Where are we?" Jahir asked.

"In the Desultar Nebula," Skold replied. "On the planet Sirocco."

He reached down and picked up a handful of sand, letting the grains run through his fingers.

"Carbon flecks and sodium powder," Skold continued. "It's a salt planet. Finding water will be impossible. If we're still stuck here come morning, we're going be mighty thirsty."

"How did you get on our dreadnought?" Ryic asked.

"Your guess is as good as mine," Skold answered. "We were taken from the Ulam's detention facility and loaded into an armored transport cube. We were meant to be delivered to an asteroid prison. But lucky for us—or maybe not so lucky—it seems we were mistakenly put on the wrong ship."

"Don't believe anything that comes out of his mouth," Kaylee said. "There's a reason he's in shockles. Or was in them, anyway."

"I'm sorry," Skold said. "I didn't realize we'd met."

"You stole from my father."

"You're going to have to be more specific. I steal from a lot of people."

"You nicked the ventilator off his ship, the *Copernicus*," Kaylee said. "Nearly suffocated everyone on board."

"Oh, yeah. That ship was supposed to be empty at the time. The itinerary said they were scheduled for an on-planet contracting meeting."

"How much did you get for it?" she asked bitterly.

"Haven't found a buyer yet. If your father's interested, I'd be willing to sell it back to him at a good price."

Kaylee spat at Skold's feet.

"Save your fluids," he said. "I told you, this is a salt planet."

"Can't I just eat her now?" Lalique asked.

"If things were different, I might say yes. But we're going to need at least one of these kids to launch a hopper ship out of this planet's designated safe haven. And there's a good chance they won't all make it to the haven alive."

Lalique pouted.

"If you're hungry, have one of these," Skold said. He opened the supply canister he'd taken off the ship and tossed her a spaste pouch. It was roughly the size of a tube of toothpaste.

"I don't eat this garbage," Lalique said, throwing the pouch to the sand.

Skold immediately retrieved it.

"There's enough sustenance inside each of these to keep us alive for days," he said. "Don't be stupid."

Suddenly the ground began to tremble beneath their feet.

"A sinkhole," Jahir said.

"I don't think so," Skold replied.

A pale appendage stretched out of the sand, moving

with incredible speed. Its leechlike mouth struck Lalique on her back, digging its circle of teeth into her. Before Lalique or anyone else could react, a horrible sucking sound was heard. By the time Jahir had aimed his sonic crossbow, it was too late. Lalique had been drained of every last drop of moisture, leaving nothing of her body but a mummified carcass of bone and fur.

Jahir let out an ear-shattering howl. "My sister!"

He unloaded a volley of sonic blasts, but most seemed to bounce off the beast's rock-hard exoskeleton.

Zachary and the others were backing away as the rest of the creature emerged. It looked like an eyeless octopus, but with nine long sucker tubes extending from its body. The crosshairs of Zachary's lensicon locked in. He blinked twice.

LIFE-FORM: DEHYDRA

THIS NATIVE OF PLANET SIROCCO IS NOTABLE FOR ITS ABILITY TO DRAIN MOISTURE FROM ITS PREY THROUGH EACH OF ITS NINE SIPHON TENDRILS.

IT SPENDS MOST OF ITS TIME BENEATH THE SAND, LIVING ON WATER STORED IN ITS WARM, TENDER BELLY.

Zachary would have read further, but one of the dehydra's suckers was snaking toward him. He grabbed the sonic crossbow that had dropped from Lalique's hand and took a shot at the creature. The beam of sound hit the attacking sucker but only stunned it for a moment. The sucker resumed its pursuit of Zachary with single-minded determination.

And the creature's other eight arms appeared just as thirsty, setting their sights on the rest of the group.

"It wants to suck us all dry," Zachary called out.

"I didn't think it would be giving out kisses," Skold replied.

Instead of running away, Kur'tuo turned to the appendage coming up behind him. He slashed at it with his forearm, cutting the mouth clear off. The severed appendage fell to the ground and began writhing.

Kur'tuo made a series of loud clicks at the dehydra.

"Cursing at it isn't going to help," Skold said.

The chopped sucker was already regenerating itself, forming a new mouth and growing new teeth.

"We're not going to be able to kill this thing," Kaylee said. "And I'm not sure we can outrun it, either."

"Maybe we can distract it," Zachary said.

"With what?" Ryic asked.

"Vreeks." Zachary looked to the subzero freezer that had been thrown from the wreckage. It was only fifty yards off, but there would be no way to get to it with the dehydra standing in his way. Even Ryic wouldn't be able to stretch far enough to unlatch the freezers.

"Somebody cover me," Zachary said. "I'll try to make a run for it."

"Use your warp glove, kid," Skold replied. "Haven't they taught you anything at Indigo 8?"

His warp glove! Of course! Zachary was about to find out if his Starbounder training was worth anything at all. Two calculations had to be made first. Direction was easy—he'd just point at the desired target. As for distance, the more he rotated his wrist clockwise, the farther away the hole would appear. Zachary thrust his hand forward, twisting his wrist, and pointed his index finger. A black disc formed precisely as he aimed. He reached through and watched as a second hole materialized fifty yards away, just inches from the freezer. His gloved hand emerged from that hole and gripped the latch, opening it.

Then Zachary pulled his warp glove back to his side.

Vreeks immediately squirmed out of the freezer, charging for the warm belly of the dehydra. The giant Siroccan beast spun its attention to the slimy critters and the open freezer behind them. Three of the appendages dived into the icebox and started to soak up every remnant of frost inside, while the other six arms began sucking the life out of the vreeks.

"Follow me," Skold said, running toward a rock-covered ridge in the distance. "Hopefully that thing doesn't know how to climb."

The others took off behind him. They sprinted for the rocks and didn't stop, but Zachary turned back to see the vreeks shriveling up one by one. He moved even faster, not wanting to suffer their fate. Unlike the chase down to the bonfire at Indigo 8, which had been filled with giddy excitement, this was a run with decidedly different stakes—life or death. And there was nothing fun about it.

Finally they reached a safe hiding spot behind the rocks on the ridge.

"Now what?" Ryic asked, catching his breath.

"This is an IPDL-registered planet," Skold said. "Every

one of them has a safe haven that houses an emergency hopper ship with enough fuel to get to the nearest space station."

"How do we find one of these safe havens?" Zachary asked.

"That's where you come in," Skold said. "Each Starbounder's warp glove has a built-in homing device that will guide its wielder to the closest one. From this point on, we're a team. At least until we don't need you alive anymore."

"If anything happens to us, life in an asteroid prison will seem like a vacation compared to what the IPDL will do to you," Zachary said. "My name is Zachary Night. My great-great-grandfather was Frederick Night. This warp glove on my hand right now is the same one Gerald Night wore in the Battle of Siarnaq. My brother, Jacob Night—"

Skold cut him off.

"Look, kid, the only night I'm scared of is the one that's coming when those two suns set. Now let's move."

270°

0°

0°

**LIFE-FORM:
DEHYDRA**

THIS NATIVE OF PLANET SI-
ROCCO IS NOTABLE FOR ITS ABIL-
ITY TO DRAIN MOISTURE FROM
ITS PREY THROUGH EACH OF ITS
NINE SIPHON TENDRILS.

«SIX»

Beads of perspiration dripped down Zachary's cheek, then fell to the desert sand below. Zachary had already stripped off the custodial jumpsuit and was down to his T-shirt and cargo pants, but that didn't stop the sweat from coming. Each drop that hit the salty ground was immediately swarmed by inch-long insects. Zachary's lensicon had identified them several miles back as sweat mites, Siroccan parasites that fed off a larger organism's secretions of sweat, blood, or mucus.

Using the Starbounders' warp gloves as their guide to the safe haven, the three alien fugitives, alongside Zachary, Kaylee, and Ryic, traveled across the desolate landscape. The first sun had already set and the second was nearing the horizon. It was hard to tell how many hours had passed.

"If I hadn't come to Indigo 8, I'd be starting classes this week," Zachary said. "I wonder who got my locker. It was pretty good real estate. Right next to Olivia Nichols."

"I don't know about you," Kaylee said, "but stranded on a salt planet in the middle of the outerverse with three alien fugitives . . . that's an upgrade from my school."

"You must have had *some* friends you didn't want to say good-bye to," Zachary said.

"I wasn't exactly a friendship-bracelet kind of girl."

"Well, I felt terrible having to lie to my friends. Telling them my parents were sending me to boarding school. What am I supposed to say when I go home for the holidays?" Zachary looked down at the gash in his forearm from the crash. "That I got half my arm torn off in the Pine Lake Academy computer lab?"

"You live on a strange planet, kid," Skold said. "There aren't too many places left in the galaxy that hide the truth about the outerverse from their people. Of course, in Earth's case, I don't entirely disagree. It seems that most of your species isn't ready for all this."

"Are you sure we're heading in the right direction?" Jahir asked impatiently.

Skold grabbed Ryic's arm and looked at the palm of his glove. One edge of the circle pulsed brighter, signaling the direction to follow. The faster the light oscillated, the closer the glove's wielder was to the intended destination, but the pulse was fairly slow. "We're on track," Skold said. "Trust me." By the way Jahir was snarling, it was clear that he didn't, but Skold didn't care. "You three should probably have something to eat," he said, tossing Kaylee the supply canister.

She caught it in her hand, unlatched the top, and passed Zachary and Ryic a spaste pouch. Then she pulled one out for herself.

"What flavor did you get?" Ryic asked Zachary.

"Flavor?" Zachary replied. This was his first encounter with the unusual food substitute.

"It says on the bottom of your pouch."

Zachary flipped his over and read the print on the foil.

"A hard-boiled egg," he said.

"I got sausage-and-pepperoni pizza," Ryic replied. "Want to trade?"

"You want to trade sausage-and-pepperoni pizza for a hard-boiled egg?" Zachary asked.

"I know it is decidedly to my advantage," Ryic said apologetically.

"For you, buddy, I'll do it."

The two swapped spaste pouches, and Ryic squeezed a bit of his into his mouth. He swallowed, looked satisfied, and confirmed that by saying, "Delicious."

Zachary unscrewed the cap of his spaste and brought the open end to his lips. Then he squeezed out a mouthful. While it had the texture of toothpaste, it did taste remarkably like a sausage-and-pepperoni pizza.

"Mine's pretty good, too," he said enthusiastically. More surprising, he felt full after one bite.

Without warning, Kaylee dropped the supply canister and kicked it away from her.

"Something's in there," she said.

Everyone looked down at the circular metal container as it moved on its own, shaking and rattling back and forth. Skold aimed his photon cannon, but before he fired, a tiny baby vreek emerged, with four long feelers that looked too big for its body. Although it didn't have eyes or a face, it seemed lost and scared.

Skold lowered his weapon.

"Let's keep moving," he said.

The group started up again, leaving the sluglike creature behind. Immediately the sweat mites that had been following them surrounded it. The vreek let out a scared squeak.

Kaylee paused, then doubled back. She reached down and lifted the baby vreek into her hand.

"What are you doing?" Zachary asked.

"We can't just leave it here," she said.

"Why not? Have you seen what that cute little thing turns into?"

"I'm taking it," Kaylee said, slipping the creature into one of the pockets on her jumpsuit. "Don't worry," she whispered to the baby vreek. "I have a pet chinchilla at home."

The group continued its swift pace forward. Skold led the way out in front of them, pounding the shockle on his left wrist with a rock, trying to break it off like he had already done with the one on his right. Unsuccessful, he removed a pair of magnetic tweezers from his pocket and began to jimmy the shockle's locking mechanism. But instead of unfastening it, all the tweezers did was ignite a flash of light. Even from where Zachary was standing, the neutron burst made him see stars.

"Unless you want to go blind, I'd keep your distance," warned Skold, who seemed unaffected by the blast and tried the tweezers again.

"So, what did the IPDL finally get you for, anyway?" Kaylee asked, turning her gaze from the shockles.

"I believe the technical charge was intergalactic grand theft larceny."

"Must have been a pretty big score to get you life in an asteroid prison," Kaylee said.

"Oh, it was big," Skold said. "The kind of big that buys you your own solar system."

"Well, it's a shame that didn't work out for you," Kaylee said.

"Maybe next time you'll find yourself some smarter accomplices," Zachary said under his breath.

Skold eyed Kur'tuo and Jahir, who were keeping pace alongside him.

"Who, them? I run my operations solo. We were just cell mates in the detention facility at Indigo 8. Once we get off this planet, we won't be sending each other holiday cards."

"And I thought we'd grown so close," Jahir said.

"For someone who's not from Earth, you certainly talk like someone who is," Zachary said to Skold.

"I was trained as a diplomat," Skold replied. "In order to better communicate with your species, I had to learn to mimic the local vernacular and customs."

"If they weren't part of your crew, what crimes did they commit?" Zachary asked.

Jahir answered for himself. "An interstellar peacekeeping team visited my home moon bringing food rations. But Lalique and I chose to eat the peacekeeping team instead."

Kur'tuo let out a series of clicks.

"He says he was imprisoned for destroying a peaceful plant," Skold translated.

"That doesn't sound so bad," Ryic said. "I have been guilty of herbicide on occasion. I especially like this dish you call Cobb salad."

Kur'tuo clicked angrily.

"I'm sorry," Skold said, correcting himself. "Peaceful *planet*."

The group came up over another ridge. Ahead, a glimmering lake stretched for miles into the distance, with thin silver jetties crisscrossing it.

"I thought you said there wasn't any water here." Ryic was looking curiously down the slope at the crystal-clear liquid.

The sweat mites that had been following them suddenly reversed course and scattered in the opposite direction.

"I'm guessing that's not water," Skold said.

The six reached the edge of the lake. Zachary glanced down and was tempted to drop to his knees and lap up the liquid like a thirsty dog. But the sound of sizzling broke his daydream. He looked at the tip of his friction boot and saw that it had touched the still pool, causing the rubber material to bubble and disintegrate. He quickly stepped back.

"Hydrochloric acid," Skold said. "An entire lake of it."

Skold grabbed Ryic by the wrist and checked the pulsing light on his warp glove. "The safe haven is on the other side of the lake." Skold's eyes shifted to the narrow silver jetties that rose above its surface. Unaffected by the corrosive power of the acid, they had naturally formed like sandbars at a beach. "We'll have to cross using these jetties. They must be composed of some kind of metal that isn't harmed by the acid. Of course I won't be the one testing it out." Skold pushed Zachary forward. "You will."

The entire group went silent as he put his left foot onto the path. Just a boot's width wide, with hydrochloric acid calmly hugging either side, the jetty hardly looked safe. All of Zachary's concentration was focused on his own two feet. Never before had he been so careful with his steps: left heel to right toe, right heel to left toe. Just a moment of distraction, the tiniest slipup, and he could be without a foot or leg.

But Skold was right. The jetty was solid enough to cross. And the others all followed behind Zachary

They got a quarter of the way across the lake and found themselves on a large island of the silver metal. Multiple jetties split off from it, each one snaking through the sea of acid, but which would lead to the other side? No matter how hard he strained, Zachary couldn't get a clear enough view of the maze of silver to really be sure.

"We'll go down each one if we have to," Skold said.

He set off on the center path, and the others followed.

"My dad used to take my brother and me out fishing," Zachary said to Kaylee and Ryic. "We'd go early in the morning when the water was calm. It looked like glass, just like this. Jacob would let me hook the worms so I wouldn't feel left out when he caught all the fish."

Zachary felt a gentle breeze blow across the acid lake and took relief in the momentary cool. Kaylee did, too, leaning her head back and letting the wind drift through her hair. But Kur'tuo, who was tailing behind her, had no patience for even the slightest pause. He shoved her forward, clicking angrily. The force sent Kaylee stumbling toward the edge of the jetty, and she nearly fell into the hydrochloric pool. Luckily, Zachary reached back and gripped her arm, steadying her.

"Didn't your mother ever teach you manners?" Kaylee asked Kur'tuo, trying to restrain her anger.

Kur'tuo responded with a series of clicks.

"He says he was one of a thousand eggs," Skold translated. "His mother was busy."

The breeze picked up, making tiny ripples in the acid. In the distance, billowing clouds of sand were churning, heading toward them.

"We need to get across this lake," Zachary said. "Fast."

"He's right," Skold said. "Once that salt storm reaches us, those ripples are going to turn into full-blown waves. And these thin strips of land won't be able to protect us."

One after the other, Skold, Ryic, Zachary, Kaylee, Kur'tuo, and Jahir began to run, no longer having the luxury of taking each step with care. Although they were moving quickly, the oncoming salt storm was moving faster. As the wind got stronger, Zachary could feel flakes of salt hitting his lips, making them pucker.

They reached a second island, this one with a tall, thin silver spire at its center. Waves of acid were now cresting and breaking over the jetties.

"We're trapped," Zachary said.

The six of them huddled closer, moving in toward the spire as the acid level continued rising. The salt storm was now raging all around them, causing Zachary's eyes to sting. He felt a burning sensation on the back of his leg, where a spray of hydrochloric acid had eaten away at his pants and was sizzling against his calf.

All the Night family stories ended with epic battles won and medals being earned for acts of bravery. But Zachary couldn't remember a single tale ending like this.

"We sure could use my dad's fishing boat right about now," Zachary said. "Of course, the acid would eat through it pretty quickly."

Kaylee, who had been examining the spire, got a spark in her eyes. "What if we make our own boat?" She rapped her fist against the metal surface. "It's hollow."

"We'll have to break it off from the base and split it open," Zachary said, seeing her plan. "Then we can ride it to the other side of the lake like a canoe."

Skold must have thought it was a good idea because he had already loaded his photon cannon and was firing at the spot where the spire met the island.

The rest of them stood back as the blasts began to shake the spire. After a series of rapid shots, Skold's cannon finally tipped it.

"Kur'tuo, cut the spire from end to end," Kaylee shouted.

The alien made several clicks and turned away.

"He says no one gives orders to Kur'tuo," Skold translated. "Especially little girls." Kaylee stared daggers at Skold. "His words. Not mine." Then taking aim with his cannon, Skold sent blasts along the top edge of the spire.

The waves were getting bigger now, crashing onto the island. Their makeshift canoe was finished just in time.

"Get it into the lake," Kaylee cried over the roar of the storm.

Everyone gathered around one end and pushed the spire along the island to the edge of the lake. Now Zachary just hoped that it would float. With a final thrust, the metal skiff slid into the choppy acid and remained buoyant.

"Pile in," Skold said.

One by one they climbed aboard, and once all six were inside they let the wind and waves carry them away from the island. Flecks of acid continued to spray the inside of the boat, eating away at their clothes and burning their flesh. More problematic was the fact that the escape vessel was starting to sink. It was carrying too much weight.

Kur'tuo grunted out a series of clicks.

"He's right," Skold said. "Looks like maximum occupancy is five." He eyed the three Starbounders-in-training. "So, which one of you feels like taking a dip?"

But Kur'tuo wasn't waiting for any volunteers. He thrust out an arm at Ryic, gripping him by the shirt. Just before he chucked him overboard, Kaylee's right foot flew into Kur'tuo's abdomen with enough force to knock him straight off the boat. The alien's bug-like eyes went even wider as he tumbled into the acid, his body melting into a green pool with an awful hissing sound. The spire immediately rose up again, no longer on the verge of sinking.

"I guess he was just feeling selfless," Kaylee said without a hint of remorse.

The silver vessel lurched at the whims of the storm. With no oar to propel them and no one volunteering to use their arms as paddles, they bobbed along the acid waves until the salt storm blew itself out and the sky became clear again. When the tip of the canoe ran aground on the opposite end of the lake, they got out in time to see Sirocco's second sun dipping below the horizon. It was dark in an instant. The thin atmosphere couldn't hold a sunset.

Skold walked up beside Ryic and took a look at the pulsing light on his warp glove to gauge their distance from the safe haven.

"We're still miles away," he said. "As much as I wanted to get to the hopper ship today, I think traveling at night will be too dangerous. I'd hate to accidentally step into a sinkhole or walk into a dehydra we don't even know is there. Let's stop here. It seems as good a spot as any."

Zachary looked around. He saw nothing but salty dunes in every direction. No shelter. No caves to curl up in. They'd have to spend the night exposed to the elements. Back home, when Zachary went camping, at least he had a tent and a sleeping bag. Here they had no equipment. Sleeping under the stars would mean just that. Lying with their backs on the sand and their faces to the sky.

Skold took a seat on a nearby rock and took out his magnetic tweezers, still intent on freeing his wrist from the shockle. Jahir pulled the loose skin hanging from his bones around him like a blanket and curled up to go to sleep.

Zachary, Ryic, and Kaylee were left to fend for themselves. Zachary's lips were badly cracked and he could barely conjure up enough saliva to moisten them.

"I say we wait until they're both asleep and then make a run for it," Kaylee whispered. "We can find that hopper ship and jump to the nearest space station."

"Weaponless and on our own?" Ryic asked.

"Killed by the elements or killed by them," Kaylee said.

Out of the corner of his eye, Zachary could see neutron bursts as Skold attempted to remove the shockle.

"I think we'd be better off pretending to be on their side a little longer," Zachary argued, his voice hoarse. "Then we seize our moment."

"I'm with him," Ryic said.

Kaylee might not have agreed, but she seemed to respect the fact that she was outvoted.

No spot seemed better than any other for sleeping, so Zachary, Kaylee, and Ryic lay down on the ground where they were, side by side. They stared up at the swirl of stars dotting the greenish space clouds of the distant Stringer Nebula.

"Back home, I would stargaze with my numerical predecessor, Jengi 1,174,830," Ryic said suddenly. "I miss her very much."

"Is she like your sister or something?" Kaylee asked.

"Not exactly. We do not have siblings on Klenarog, at least not in the way you do on Earth. Every member of my species is birthed from the Origin Pool, primordial waters that elders return to at the end of their lives. From their dissolved remains new Klenarogians emerge. We are all given a name and number, and our destinies are chosen at random."

"Did you grow up in a house or have a mom and dad?" Zachary asked.

"I was raised in the youth barracks, under the tutelage of the planet's finest mentors. Love and caring were doled out in equal rations, the same as meals and showers."

"Well, at least you could never be disappointed that way," Kaylee said.

"I guess I was one of the lucky ones," Zachary said. "My family has always been there for me."

The three lay silently for a moment.

"Do you think anyone is looking for us?" Ryic asked.

"Sure, they might be looking," Kaylee said. "It's finding us that's the tricky part. I once saw this show on the Discovery Channel that said if someone goes overboard on a cruise ship at night, the odds of being rescued are one in a million. Now picture that instead of being lost at sea, you're lost in an infinite universe."

"What do you think they've told our parents?" Zachary asked Kaylee.

"Probably that there was an accident," Kaylee said. "Or that they lost communication with our ship."

Zachary's chest immediately tightened. He had a horrible feeling that he would never see his family again. How was he supposed to get his friends out of this mess? When was Jacob going to drop in from wherever it was he was on assignment to save them? Or would they be spending the rest of their short lives here on Sirocco? Kingston was sounding pretty good right about now.

° ° °

Zachary had been falling in and out of sleep for what felt like hours. Every time he drifted off, his dreams took him to waterfalls or mountain springs. But the mental mirages left him just as thirsty as before. Then he felt a drop of water land on his forehead. This was no dream. Was it raining?

Zachary's eyes peeled open to find Jahir standing over him, drooling from his open mouth. As the gaunt alien bared his wolfish teeth and lunged, Zachary acted on instinct alone, rolling out of the way.

He screamed for help; at least he tried to. But his throat had become so dry, all that came out was a scratchy, barely audible wheeze. Kaylee and Ryic slept right through it.

"I hate to go to bed on an empty stomach." Jahir licked his lips as he circled his prey. Zachary could already picture Jahir burying those long fangs in his flesh.

Clenching his fists, he realized he was still wearing his glove. Then, in the dim starlight he spotted one of the sonic crossbows lying near the sleeping Skold. Acting fast, Zachary opened a warp hole. He grabbed the crossbow, pulling it to his side. Without hesitating he took aim at Jahir and pulled the trigger. But no beam of sound shot out from the crossbow. Zachary looked down to see salt clogging the firing mechanism. When his eyes flicked back up to his enemy, Jahir was smiling.

The fugitive pounced, clawing at Zachary's face and

pinning him on his back. Jahir was closing in for the kill. Zachary used all his strength to push the beast but was unsuccessful. Jahir's teeth were moving toward Zachary's neck when a photon bolt struck him in the back of the head, felling him to the ground instantly. Zachary shoved the lifeless alien off him to see Skold standing with photon cannon in hand.

"It wasn't going to be long before I was on the menu, too," Skold said.

The blast had awakened Ryic and Kaylee. They scrambled to their feet.

"What happened?" Ryic asked, still disoriented.

"Jahir was looking for a midnight snack," Zachary whispered hoarsely, wiping blood from the deep scratches on his cheeks.

"Zachary, are you okay?" Kaylee asked, moving toward him to help.

"I've been in fights before," Zachary croaked. "Granted, most of them weren't with aliens who looked like the Big Bad Wolf's ugly cousin."

Skold was digging a hole beside Jahir's body. The shockle still dangled from his left wrist.

"You really think he deserves a proper burial?" Kaylee asked, making it obvious she didn't.

"I just don't want to be stuck smelling him all night," Skold said. "Now go back to sleep. We still have a few hours before dawn."

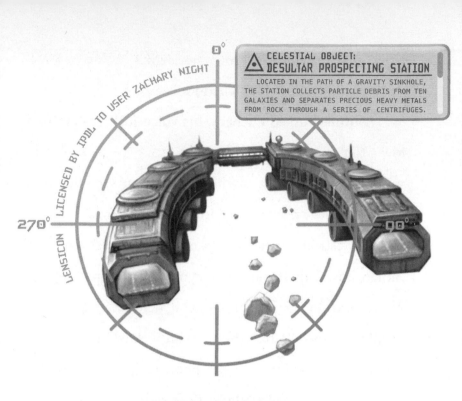

270°

0°

CELESTIAL OBJECT:
DESULTAR PROSPECTING STATION
LOCATED IN THE PATH OF A GRAVITY SINKHOLE, THE STATION COLLECTS PARTICLE DEBRIS FROM TEN GALAXIES AND SEPARATES PRECIOUS HEAVY METALS FROM ROCK THROUGH A SERIES OF CENTRIFUGES.

«SEVEN»

The first sun of Sirocco had risen, and the four remaining survivors of the *Dreadnought Epsilon* crash wasted no time. Guided by the compass in Ryic's warp glove, they walked for hours over the increasingly hot sand. According to the pulsing light, they were getting close to the safe haven—and the emergency hopper ship docked inside it.

Zachary walked beside Kaylee, who was letting the

baby vreek crawl up and down her arm.

"Sputnik, that tickles," said Kaylee.

"Sputnik?" asked Zachary, his voice still scratchy and low. "You gave it a name?"

"He reminded me of the old Russian satellite, with those four little needles sticking out of his back."

Skold strode ahead of them, preoccupied with the indigo box with the infinity symbol on it that he had removed from the dreadnought. It made Zachary think of all those people back home who walked around with their noses buried in their cell phones. Then Skold pulled a thin wire from the artificial flesh of his right wrist and inserted it into a tiny hole on the side of the box.

"What are you doing?" Zachary asked, slightly sickened by the sight.

"Uploading the data from the ship's starbox," Skold replied.

"*That's* the starbox?"

Zachary had imagined the dreadnought's heart and brain to be a giant supercomputer, not something smaller than an iPhone.

"There's only one thing more valuable than parts,"

Skold said. "Knowledge."

"What, do you have an internal hard drive or something?" Kaylee asked, pointing to the wire sticking out of Skold's wrist.

"This shell comes with all kinds of perks," Skold said. "I've got emergency oxygen tanks, a water filtration system, and I even sprang for all ten thousand channels of universal satellite TV. Although I have to admit, reception can be spotty."

"How did you go from diplomat to outerverse felon?" Zachary asked.

"From studying Earthlings," Skold replied. "My kind— the people of Ota Stella—don't know anything of thievery or crime. We have no personal belongings, and the welfare of one another is prized more than anything. But after many years of living among your species, seeing all of your greed and ambition, I recognized the wisdom of your ways."

"What was that?" Zachary asked.

"That taking and earning are not that different—both put money in your pocket. And that fast ships are fun." Skold gave a sly grin. "You three have been asking an awful lot of questions. Now what about you?" He eyed Kaylee. "What's with the piercings and colored hair? Daddy taking too many business trips to the outerverse? Need something to get his attention during his short stops home?"

"You don't know anything about me," Kaylee said. She walked ahead, clearly bothered.

Skold turned to Ryic.

"You're from Klenarog, right? That planet has some of the finest combatants and pilots in the known galaxies. Just never heard of them sending anyone to the IPDL. Don't they have their own fleet? Couldn't make the grade at home? So you got dumped at Indigo 8?"

At first Zachary thought Skold's provoking was off the mark, but he could tell by the way Ryic was avoiding eye contact that his taunts had touched a nerve.

Finally Skold's attention fell on Zachary.

"I'm not sure about you, kid. But something tells me you've got a long way to go before that warp glove fits you."

The words cut deep for Zachary. What he wanted more than anything was to live up to his family's legacy, but Skold was right.

"You gonna charge me for that brilliant insight?"

Zachary challenged. He had no intention of letting Skold—or Kaylee or Ryic—see any weakness in him.

"No, the first hour is free," Skold replied. "Come on, let's pick up the pace."

If the fugitive's goal had been to get them to quit asking questions, he'd succeeded. For a while the only thing that broke the silence was the sound of Sputnik cooing inside Kaylee's pocket. Then Ryic spoke.

"Look," he said, pointing into the distance.

Through the salt clouds they could spy a silver dot on the horizon reflecting the planet's two suns brightly.

"That's it, all right," Skold said. "That's where we're headed. But we've still got plenty of time to uncork all your skeletons. Now which of you is going to start sharing?"

∘ ∘ ∘

What had only been a small, gleaming dot hours earlier had now come into clear focus. It was a bunker resembling a flat-topped pyramid. A holographic flag on the top bore the IPDL symbol. The flag looked like it was flapping in the wind, but unlike an ordinary flag, it would never be destroyed by salt storms or other climatic disasters.

Skold led them to the bunker's solid front wall, where a single fist-sized indentation was the only shape on the otherwise completely smooth surface.

"Who'd like to do the honors?" Skold asked. Zachary stepped up but didn't know what he was supposed to do. "Press your warp glove against it."

Zachary activated his glove and inserted it into the spot on the wall. A magnetic force held the glove tightly in place. Then it released and one side of the building slid open. LED lights blinked on, revealing a large chamber within. Once everyone rushed inside, the open wall of the bunker automatically sealed shut behind them.

Zachary had expected to find only the hopper ship within the IPDL safe haven but was pleasantly surprised to see tanks of water lining the walls, along with emergency food rations and first aid supplies. A small spacecraft stood at the center of the bunker. It was an egg-shaped pod with oval portholes on opposite sides. No bigger than an RV, it had four giant metallic legs elevating the pod five feet off the ground. Ladderlike steps led to the door.

"Grab some water," Skold told them. "Then we can get

off this nightmare of a planet."

Zachary, Kaylee, and Ryic eagerly ran up to one of the walls, snatching empty thermoses and filling them to the brim with water from the spigots near the bottoms of the tanks. They threw back the drinks, letting the liquid flow down their dry throats. Zachary swallowed gulp after gulp. Never had water tasted so good. He began to choke even as he continued to swallow.

Kaylee pulled her mouth away from her thermos slightly but made a point of keeping it in front of her lips.

"How are we going to ditch him?" she asked quietly under her breath. "It's only a matter of time before we're on the wrong end of that photon cannon."

"He saved my life," Zachary replied, in equally hushed tones.

"We can't trust him. He'll sacrifice us the first chance he gets."

Zachary nodded. He knew she was right.

"Are you sure this isn't personal?" Ryic asked. "For what Skold did to your father?"

"I just want us to get home," Kaylee said.

They all glanced over at the fugitive, who was raiding

the first aid supplies. His photon cannon was slung across his back.

"Now's our chance," Kaylee said. "Zachary, on the count of three, use your warp glove to unlatch his shoulder harness. I'll grab the weapon once it's loose."

"What about me?" Ryic asked.

"You might want to duck behind something," Kaylee said. "In case things don't go as planned." She turned to Zachary. "One . . . two . . . three."

In unison they held out their warp gloves. Two holes opened right behind Skold. Zachary reached through the first, snapping the shoulder latch. Kaylee's hand emerged from the second and grabbed the photon cannon. By the time Skold turned around, Kaylee was pointing the weapon straight at him.

"Nice teamwork," Skold said. "Gold stars for both of you."

"Don't take another step," Kaylee warned.

Skold put his hands up slowly. "Let's talk about this." Then he took a stride toward them.

"I said don't move," Kaylee repeated.

"What are you going to do, shoot me?"

"If I have to."

Skold smiled. "All right. You win. What now?"

He stepped closer.

Kaylee pulled the trigger on the photon cannon. But the weapon didn't fire. She tried again, but no beam of superheated light shot forth. Zachary fought off a sickly feeling. The plan had backfired.

"I took the cartridge out before we left this morning," Skold said. "I stopped trusting you after you kicked Kur'tuo into that acid lake."

He reached out and took back the photon cannon, then replaced the cartridge with a loaded clip.

"Now get on the ship," he said, waving his cannon toward the steps.

Zachary, Ryic, and Kaylee did as they were told, and found another fist-sized indentation at the door. This time Kaylee stuck her warp glove inside. The pod opened, allowing all four of them to enter.

The inside of the ship was sparse, with a half dozen seats that made a circle around a control panel. There was little else. This was the planet's life raft, built for survival, not comfort. They all buckled in, and Sputnik climbed out to look around.

"Launch us out of here," Skold said. "Any of your gloves will do the trick."

Zachary reached out and inserted his glove into the lone indentation on the control panel. The door closed with a surprisingly loud bang, startling Sputnik, who ducked back into Kaylee's pocket.

Zachary looked out the porthole but could only see one of the haven's walls. He heard the bunker's roof retract and felt the hopper ship's four mechanical legs begin to move. They seemed to bend at the knees before vaulting upward, taking to the air. The force of the jump pushed Zachary down into his seat, like a spatula pressing down on a pancake. It felt as if he would flatten at any moment. The pod sprang through the open roof of the bunker, and once it was several hundred feet above Sirocco's salty surface, the engines kicked in. The hopper ship soared higher and higher, fighting the planet's gravity before freeing itself from Sirocco's atmosphere and rocketing into space.

A small holographic image projected over the console, displaying a path from Sirocco to the Desultar Prospecting Station. Estimated time until arrival was 00:22:41—less than twenty-three minutes.

Skold looked as if he was typing on an invisible keyboard in midair. Clearly he had executed some kind of remote command, because after a moment, a message appeared on the holographic display reading, *Request for Clandestine Approach Accepted*. The lighting in the ship immediately changed color to a cool blue.

"What does that mean?" Zachary asked, wondering what the fugitive was up to.

"It means the ship will be cloaked and our arrival at the prospecting station won't be announced. Probably best if I don't have a welcoming party."

As the estimated arrival time dwindled to just a few minutes, Zachary alternated between staring out at the cosmos and nervously eyeing the barrel of Skold's photon cannon. He feared that once they landed and Skold got ahold of his own ship, they'd be of no use to him. Then what would prevent the ruthless space convict from killing them as easily as he'd killed Jahir?

"That must be it." Ryic's voice shook Zachary from his thoughts. He saw that his friend was pointing out the porthole to a space station.

Curved like a boomerang, it had two halves connected by a single walkway. It looked big enough to fit half of Kingston inside. A river of space rocks was hurtling toward the center of the station. Large asteroids and comets tumbled into an opening beneath the walkway in a steady flow.

Fixing the crosshairs of his lensicon on the station, Zachary blinked twice.

⚠ **CELESTIAL OBJECT:**
DESULTAR PROSPECTING STATION

LOCATED IN THE PATH OF A GRAVITY SINKHOLE, THE STATION COLLECTS PARTICLE DEBRIS FROM TEN GALAXIES AND SEPARATES PRECIOUS HEAVY METALS FROM ROCK THROUGH A SERIES OF CENTRIFUGES. THE EXTRACTED ORE IS ONE OF THE MOST VALUABLE SOURCES OF MINERAL WEALTH IN THE KNOWN OUTERVERSE.

THIS IPDL-SANCTIONED FACILITY IS CONSIDERED A SAFE PLACE TO DOCK.

What about those accompanied by an armed felon, Zachary wondered? Was it safe for them?

The hopper ship was nearing the station, and the ship's mechanical legs were now stretching out beyond the pod like tentacles preparing to latch on to something.

Through the porthole, Zachary could see spacecraft large and small, docked along the outside of the station. Swarms of flying motorcycles manned by aux-bots zipped among them. One stopped and began to repair holes in the station's hull.

The holographic display read *Approaching Auxiliary Terminal* as they neared the end of the prospecting station. Zachary watched as their ship slipped between a decrepit fuel tanker and a rusty dreadnought. Its legs reached out and gripped the footholds of a station docking portal.

"Don't try anything funny," Skold warned them as he concealed the photon cannon beneath his jacket. "Once I secure a ship that can bound me past the Asteroid Curtain, I'll set you free."

The top of the pod opened, and the group floated into what Zachary's lensicon identified as an atmospheric atrium, a small isolated room where gravity could be gradually adjusted to acclimate new visitors to the station. Zachary felt his feet sink slowly to the floor as the sensation of zero gravity disappeared. By the time the process had finished, it felt as if the gravity was even stronger here than on Earth. His legs were straining slightly under the weight of his own body mass.

"It feels like I'm carrying a pillowcase loaded with bricks." Zachary flexed his leg muscles, trying to adjust to the unusual feeling.

"This is what Klenarog feels like all the time." Ryic was smiling and stretching his arms and legs. "You'll get used to it."

Zachary took a couple of strained steps. Walking was an effort, and he was glad they didn't have to go any faster.

Skold approached a locked doorway leading into the corridors of the prospecting station. He pointed to an indentation in the wall, but Zachary already knew what he was supposed to do. He stuck his gloved hand inside, and the door retracted into the floor.

They emerged into the station's docking terminal, which was so busy with bustling workers and residents that no one seemed to notice their arrival. The vast majority of them were a short, broad-shouldered species of alien. Their facial features were similar to a human's, but their eyes were bigger and their ears smaller. The rest of the crowd was made up of other odd humanoid creatures. It didn't seem like Zachary, Kaylee, Ryic, and Skold would have any difficulty blending in as they passed from the terminal into the station's dining hub. This portion of the space station reminded Zachary of the mall food court by his house, only the vendors weren't selling tacos and pretzels. Their stands lined the halls, peddling foul-smelling soups and exotic fruits. There was even one food stand offering plates of meat that were still on fire.

Skold began leading them through the crowded market, pushing Zachary with the back of his hand. As they passed an algae stand, Ryic couldn't contain himself. He stopped for a moment to sniff in the pungent odor. The smell reminded Zachary of a wet swimsuit that had been sitting in a closet for a week, but Ryic was clearly enjoying it.

"There's nothing quite like the smell of fresh fungus drizzled with plutonium flakes," he said, still sniffing.

"As appetizing as that sounds, we need to keep moving," Skold said. He led the group through the inside of the space station to a directional kiosk tucked between a pay-by-the-minute shower stall and a friction-boot repair shop.

Skold waved his hand in front of the kiosk, and the motion-sensitive screen displayed a map showing an overview of the entire Desultar Prospecting Station. There were the two curved halves of the station connected by the single walkway Zachary had seen from space. A small marker indicated their current location on the far eastern end. Skold pointed across to the other side.

"That's where the bounder ships are," Skold said. "My ticket beyond the Indigo Divide."

"Indigo Divide?" Zachary asked.

"It's a smugglers' term. Means somewhere the IPDL can't touch me, somewhere outside their jurisdiction. I've got a moon past the Asteroid Curtain that's my personal chop shop. Ships and parts. Be nice and I'll give you my business card. Now get a move on."

They entered what looked like a factory floor, where broad-shouldered aliens manipulated robotic arms to break apart larger space debris. Farther down the line, others were running the cracked rocks through water, and any gleaming bits that were found were chipped out and placed on a conveyor belt. The noise was deafening, with constant clanging and cracking. Their path followed the conveyor belt into a different room, where the most valuable bits of metal—capendium—were plucked off and transferred into lockboxes. IPDL officers of every alien race then secured the boxes and carried them away.

Zachary was straining his face muscles to catch the attention of the uniformed officers without saying anything.

"If they try to take me, I can't help it if you get caught in the crossfire," Skold said quietly.

The threat was enough to keep the three Starbounders-in-training and Sputnik silent. They crossed through unnoticed, exiting the refinery and moving into the living quarters. They were walking swiftly now—at least, as swiftly as they could with the heavier gravity—passing another kiosk, which indicated they were nearing the walkway to the other side of the prospecting station. They reached a long hallway and found themselves approaching a guard post where a line of people waited. Skold slowed to a stop. It was clear that warp gloves alone weren't going to be enough to get them past this point.

"Please wait in line for your cranial DNA identification scan," a guard called out.

Anyone crossing through had a handheld electronic device, roughly the size of a thermometer, waved in front of their forehead. It was only a brief inconvenience if the device lit up orange, but if the reading turned up blue, the individual being scanned was immediately cuffed in shockles and dragged away.

"Looks like we need to take a detour." Skold pulled the young Starbounders out of the hallway.

"You saw the map," Zachary said. "The walkway is the only way to get across."

"From the inside," Skold replied.

He was guiding them toward an emergency exit, where a ladder led down to a sealed door.

"Are you crazy?" Kaylee asked. "Executing an untethered space walk?"

"Don't they teach you anything at Indigo 8?" Skold replied.

"We've only been there a week," Ryic said.

"Well, nothing beats on-the-fly training."

He ushered them down the ladder and unlatched the

door. They stepped into another atmospheric atrium. This one had a wall full of off-planet bio regulators and what appeared to be hi-tech rock-climbing equipment.

"Everyone gear up," Skold ordered. "Grab a magnetic grappling hook and a bio regulator."

Zachary, Kaylee, and Ryic equipped themselves. Kaylee gave a reassuring pat to Sputnik, who was sticking his head out of her pocket.

"You're going to need to hold your breath for a few minutes," she said. "Think you can do that, Sputnik?"

The vreek let out a *meep*, seeming to understand.

Zachary inserted one of the clear mouthpieces between his lips. As his mouth formed a seal around the breathing apparatus, he felt a whoosh of pure oxygen enter his lungs. With his first breath, the bio regulator formed a repulsion barrier around him, just like his lensicon said it would.

"Look," Ryic said, his word garbled by the device held fast in his jaw.

Zachary turned to see that Ryic was trying to clap his hands together, but no matter how hard he pushed, the unseen barrier kept them an inch apart.

Skold held a pair of grappling hooks in his hand but didn't wear a regulator.

"Where's your mouthpiece?" Zachary asked.

"Don't need it. I told you I've got internal oxygen tanks," Skold replied. "Now remember, I need at least one of you alive on the other side, so try not to die out there."

"Thanks for the pep talk," Zachary said.

Skold prompted Zachary to punch a button, which he did. First the gravity in the chamber disappeared, then the air was sucked out. A heavy door leading to the vacuum of space slid open. The four drifted through, weightless, each holding a magnetic grappling hook.

The first thing Zachary noticed was the silence. The spaceships that passed by above and beyond them, the comets and asteroids bouncing off the side of the space station, the blades and grinders of the prospectors' mining operation. None of it made a noise. Zachary remembered learning that in space, without molecules of air, sound didn't exist. But he hadn't really comprehended it until now.

The second thing Zachary noticed was how tiny he felt. Of course, infinite cosmos in every direction would probably make anyone feel insignificant.

Skold signaled with his hands for the three to watch him. Using his mag hook, he latched on to a distant spot on the side of the space station and started to pull himself along the rim toward the thin walkway, motioning for them to follow.

Large space rocks flowed into the whirling machinery under the walkway, and the closer they got to the center, the stronger the tug of the gravity channel became. As tiny asteroid particles flew in Zachary's direction, he braced himself, but the bio regulator's force field deflected any incoming debris.

Zachary squeezed his fingers extra tight around the grappling hook's fiberglass rope and struggled to keep his footing. Skold clearly had experience with this kind of escape. He was cruising ahead. In front of Zachary, Kaylee managed to keep pace with the fugitive. Behind him, Ryic . . . was gone. Only his mag hook remained, attached to the ship's surface.

It took a moment for Zachary to comprehend what was happening. He wanted to scream out for Ryic. He even thought he did. But as much as his lungs vibrated, no one reacted to his call. Zachary searched frantically before spotting Ryic drifting slowly toward the river of rocks. His arms flailed wildly, with nothing to grab on to and no way of propelling himself.

Zachary turned back to Skold and Kaylee, who were still completely unaware of what was happening. Unable to get their attention, Zachary knew it was up to him to do something. And he needed to do it quickly, because Ryic was getting ever closer to the prospecting station's grinders with no way to reverse his course. As effective as the force field was at deflecting rocks, it would be no match for the giant, spinning blades.

Suddenly, Zachary had a flash of the fishing trips he used to take with his dad and brother. He remembered one time when a favorite baseball cap went overboard and started flowing downstream. Jacob thought fast and sent his fishing line flying, hooking the mesh hat and reeling it in.

Zachary grabbed Ryic's grappling hook, swung, and fired. It stretched out, reaching toward Ryic's open arms. But the rope wasn't long enough. Ryic extended his arm as far as he could, but to no avail.

Kaylee and Skold had finally noticed what was going on. Kaylee's face read horror. Skold looked emotionless. He was gesturing to Zachary to forget about Ryic.

Was Skold crazy? There was no way Zachary was going to let Ryic go. He retrieved his own mag hook and leaped off the hull of the station, propelling himself straight for his friend. As he soared in space, Zachary fired Ryic's grappling hook a second time. This time, Ryic caught the other end in his hands. Now they were both drifting toward their doom, together.

Zachary turned to the ship and prepared to launch his mag hook back at the side. But before he was able to activate it, a small chunk of cosmic ice cracked against the mag hook's handle, knocking it loose from Zachary's grip and sending it tumbling toward the grinders.

Ryic had managed to pull himself to Zachary's side but seemed too overcome with panic to think clearly. Zachary knew that they needed a way to propel themselves to the station's surface, but there was nothing close enough to use as a springboard. The tug of the gravity sinkhole seemed inescapable.

Then Zachary saw the end of a magnetic grappling

hook flying toward him. He looked up to see Kaylee trying the same rescue tactic that he had. She was close enough that the hook reached him. His fingers grabbed the magnetic claw, and Kaylee reeled them back toward the ship. Zachary flooded with relief as his feet made contact with the rim and Ryic touched down beside him. They were both able to continue on their way. Zachary and Ryic shared Ryic's grappling hook, gripping one another tightly until they arrived at the other side.

Skold stopped before an emergency door to yet another atmospheric atrium. This one was beyond the walkway and the scrutiny of the DNA guard post. Zachary pressed his glove up to the indentation, and the outer door slid open. The four clambered into the safety of the atrium. Once the door closed and the whoosh of air returned, they removed their bio regulators, allowing them to talk once more. Ryic was the first to speak.

"My hand just slipped—"

"Save it for later." Skold was already waiting at the locked doorway leading back into the station. "After you open this door for me, we split ways. I'm going to have to take your warp gloves and keep you locked up in here.

They'll find you in a couple hours, but by then I'll be long gone."

With a sinking feeling, Zachary walked over and reached his warp glove—the glove that had belonged to his famous grandfather Gerald Night and the glove he was about to lose forever—out to the indentation.

"And one more thing," Skold added. "I'd stay away from—"

But before he finished, the door slid open. A dozen sonic crossbows were pointed right at them.

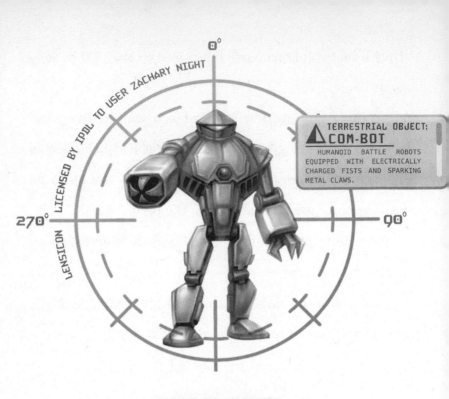

0°

270°

90°

TERRESTRIAL OBJECT:
COM-BOT

HUMANOID BATTLE ROBOTS
EQUIPPED WITH ELECTRICALLY
CHARGED FISTS AND SPARKING
METAL CLAWS.

«EIGHT»

"**S**kold Ota Stella, you're under arrest," said one of the IPDL officers taking aim. "For intergalactic grand theft larceny and attempted robbery of the Callisto perpetual energy generator. As well as hijacking, murder, and armed evasion of capture."

"You're going to have to add kidnapping to that list, too," Skold said.

He whipped out his photon cannon, and Zachary felt

it pressed up against his back before any of the officers could react. With the hard nozzle jammed into his spine, Zachary knew that all it would take was one pull of the trigger and he would never walk again. Skold huddled Ryic and Kaylee up beside Zachary and pushed them all forward.

"I'm getting on one of those ships." Skold gestured across the way to a series of docking portals where pitchforks and battle-axes were parked. The IPDL officers couldn't get a clear shot at Skold—not unless they were willing to take out one of the young Starbounders in the process.

Skold began inching out of the atmospheric atrium, using his hostages as a shield, but the officers refused to clear the way for him.

"We have authority to apprehend you regardless of the casualties," the IPDL officer told Skold.

Zachary knew what that meant. He, Ryic, and Kaylee didn't count in the big galactic picture. It was in his best interest for Skold to get on that ship.

"Drop your weapon or we'll be forced to open fire," the officer said.

Skold seemed all too willing to play this game of chicken. And Zachary wasn't going to wait to see who was going to flinch first.

He reached around the photon cannon and pulled the magnetic tweezers from Skold's jacket pocket. Pushing Kaylee out of the way, he jammed them into the shockle still clinging to Skold's left wrist.

A massive neutron burst flashed across the room, blinding every last officer. Zachary's vision was immediately clouded by the bright white light, as if he had stared directly into the sun. He felt a tug at his shirt and was quickly pulled forward.

"What was that?" Skold demanded as they hurried from the scene. "You think you were going to escape from me?"

"No," Zachary said. "It was to help you escape. I've been watching you. I saw that your eyes weren't affected by the neutron bursts back at the campsite."

Zachary could hear the disoriented shouts of IPDL officers behind him, but all he could see was a blur. He could feel Skold lift his gloved hand and hold it up to another indentation. He heard a door slide open.

"You may as well let us go," Kaylee said, coming back to Zachary's side. "We're of no use to you now. That officer said so himself."

"Haven't you ever heard of bluffing?" Skold replied. "The IPDL would never allow Starbounders-in-training to die."

Through the haze still obscuring Zachary's vision, he could tell they had boarded a ship. He just had no idea what kind. Skold pushed him down into a seat and strapped him in.

The ship began to vibrate and then took off, rocketing into space. Zachary's eyesight cleared just enough to see Skold piloting the ship toward the black disc of a space fold. If the effects of the neutron burst had worn off for the blinded IPDL officers, it was too late.

Skold and his captives had already left the galaxy behind.

° ° °

Once Zachary's vision returned to normal, he realized they were flying on a stolen battle-axe. Skold took three more bounds after escaping from the Desultar Nebula, zigzagging across the known outerverse. Coupled with their head start, the circuitous path would make tracking them next to impossible.

Zachary sat back as the ship glided through a dim expanse of space, billions of miles away from the nearest sun. Skold was studying the Kepler cartograph holographically projected on the flight-deck window.

"Kaylee, I don't want to alarm you," Ryic said, "but your face is covered in tiny black dots. Perhaps you've contracted some kind of space disease."

Zachary glanced at Kaylee, whose face appeared the same as always. Then Ryic looked down at his own hands.

"Oh, no," he exclaimed. "I have it, too!"

"Um, Ryic, I think your eyes haven't adjusted from the burst yet," Zachary said.

Ryic took a deep breath, relieved.

Skold's eyes moved from the cartograph to a control panel.

"As they say on your planet, we need to fill her up," he said. "Not enough juice to get me where I'm going. There's a void market not far from here."

He pointed to a small starless portion of the outerverse.

"I don't see anything," Zachary said.

"You're not supposed to," Skold replied.

As the battle-axe continued on in the direction that Skold had pointed, the starless patch grew in size. Zachary quickly realized that they were in fact approaching a black object camouflaging itself entirely in darkness. It didn't seem to have a single reflective surface on it.

Skold steered the ship toward the starless patch and gestured to activate the lang-link, the outerverse equivalent of radio communication. He called out in a language Zachary had never heard before. It was a combination of whirring and beeps that sounded like his dad's antique dial-up modem.

There was silence on the other end. Then the black surface of the object cracked open, revealing an entire hangar filled with spacecraft of every conceivable shape, from slick and angular to curvy and organic. Zachary recognized only a few of them.

The battle-axe flew inside, and the hangar doors sealed shut once more. The ship pulled into an empty docking space.

"Welcome to the Fringg Galaxy Void Market," echoed a robotic voice inside the cabin. "We are not liable for any of the products or services supplied here."

Skold stored his photon cannon and pocketknife in one of the underbins in the flight deck. He turned to the others.

"No weapons allowed," he said. "If you're carrying anything I don't know about, put it away now." His stare fell on Kaylee.

She pulled a voltage slingshot out from her boot and tossed it on the ground.

"Where did you get that?" Zachary asked.

"I swiped it from one of the IPDL officers after the neutron burst," she replied.

A ramp descended from the side of the ship, and Skold led the group down to the ground. They walked over to one of the hangar exits, where an outerverse being with no legs but a plethora of arms was seated in a wheeled robotic device.

"Please step on the moving platform for a routine security check," it said.

Zachary and the others proceeded onto an automated walkway.

"I feel like a piece of carry-on luggage," Zachary said

as they passed through a darkened tunnel. He was glad to reach the other side, where the same outerverse creature wheeled over to them.

"You're free to conduct whatever business it is that you've come for," said the alien. "No questions are asked here."

"We just came to fuel up," Ryic said.

"That's what everyone says," the alien replied.

They passed through a tinted sliding door and found themselves on the ground floor of a place alive with activity. The center of the space station was eight stories tall with balconies ringing each floor. Every gambling game imaginable was on display, including a fight in a giant fenced-in ring where com-bots used their mechanical claws to try to rip each other to shreds. Eager spectators were betting on the outcome, throwing down clear cubes filled with black sand.

"Those cubes are serendibite," Kaylee whispered to Zachary. "The standard outerverse currency. My father brought home a piece to show me once. Told me it was worth more than our house."

"Well, that guy looks like he just bet over a thousand

of them," Zachary said. "Someone could get very lucky tonight."

"Only if he loses," Skold said. "Anybody walking out of here with that much cash won't make it to the first space fold."

A crowd of aliens was gathered at a long counter using whirling corkscrews to crack open gigantic seashells and slurping the still-living creatures out from inside. A few who were arguing loudly and exchanging forceful shoves seemed to be drunk.

In another area, mechanical parts were being traded. Zachary spied a female figure with sandpaper skin sitting alone at a booth, examining an oddly shaped gear. Two security guards that resembled human-sized amoebas flanked her table on either side. Skold approached, and the guards immediately bulged forward, blocking his path.

"It's okay," the rough-skinned female said. The guards parted, allowing Skold to walk up to the booth. "I didn't expect to see you again so soon," she said.

"Oh, you heard about my arrest," Skold said.

"Who do you think tipped off the IPDL?"

"I wouldn't gloat, Tatania," Skold said. "That tracking mine you slipped onto my ship wasn't what got me caught."

"Pity. I was hoping I was the one who did you in."

"I need fuel," Skold said.

"Friend or enemy, I'm always willing to trade," Tatania replied.

"Trade?" Skold asked. "Wouldn't an IOU suffice?"

She let out a laugh.

"Your word is worth nothing to me."

"I thought you might say that."

Skold pulled a few parts from his jacket pocket and dropped them on the table. Zachary had seen him swipe them from the safe haven on Sirocco.

"That won't even pay for the fuel canister," Tatania said.

"What if I throw in three indentured servants?" Skold gestured back to Zachary, Kaylee, and Ryic.

"What?" Kaylee cried.

"Forced servitude is prohibited in the outerverse," Ryic said.

"Most of what I do is," Skold said.

"Too much trouble," Tatania said. "I'll take your jacket.

What is that made of, cinderbeast? You'd be amazed what rare alien rawhide fetches these days."

Skold removed the coat and threw it onto the table. Zachary's eyes darted to the hole in Skold's carapace. It had partially closed back up. Clearly the fugitive's shell came equipped with a self-repair mechanism.

"I'll have the fuel delivered to your ship," Tatania said. "Which one's yours?"

"Today I'm flying a battle-axe," Skold replied. "Docked in spot eighty-three. But tomorrow it will be up for sale. You should come visit my shop sometime. It's on Cratonis."

Tatania seemed amused. "This market is dangerous enough for me. Even I don't tread beyond the Indigo Divide."

"If you're too nervous, you can send your two blobs for you," Skold said, gesturing to her guards.

Skold stepped back and led the Starbounders away.

"You were going to sell us into slavery?" Kaylee asked.

"That was just a negotiating tactic," Skold said. "I wasn't serious."

"You fooled me," Zachary said.

Skold hurried them past a neon tattoo parlor, where

a trio of identical horn-backed aliens were having phosphorescent wings painted on their shoulder blades. He stopped in a quiet area beside a wall of sleeping pods.

"This is where we say good-bye," Skold said. "Now, I'm not big on thank-yous. . . ."

"It's easy," Kaylee said. "You just say the words. It's the least you could do after all we've done for you."

"Whoa, I was talking about *you* thanking *me*," Skold said. "Show a little gratitude. You'd all be dead right now if I hadn't gotten you this far."

"Let's just call it even," Zachary said, stepping in. "Happy to go our separate ways."

"You should be able to find passage to anywhere in the outerverse from here," Skold said.

"Well, there's only one place we plan on going," Kaylee said. "Indigo 8."

"I'd make that destination low on your list if I were you," Skold said. "That dreadnought crash was no accident. Someone inside Indigo 8 sabotaged the ship. They wanted everybody on board dead."

Zachary and his two friends looked at Skold like he was crazy.

"I don't believe you," Zachary said.

"See for yourself," Skold said.

He reached into a zippered compartment on his boot and handed Zachary the dreadnought's starbox.

"This was tampered with before we ever left Indigo 8. I think that armored transport cube I was being transferred in ended up on the ship on purpose, to make it look like we caused the crash."

Despite how elaborate Skold's story was, something didn't add up in Zachary's head.

"Believe whatever you want," Skold said, as if he could hear what Zachary was thinking.

And without another word, he turned and walked back into the market, disappearing among the crowd.

"Well, we need to find a long-range lang-link and get in touch with Director Madsen," Kaylee said.

"What about what Skold just told us?" Zachary asked.

"Everything that comes out of his mouth has an ulterior motive," Kaylee replied. "You really trust him? Two minutes ago he was ready to trade us for fuel."

It was hard for Zachary and Ryic to argue with that. Zachary pocketed the starbox, and the three of them began their search for a way to contact Indigo 8. They neared a large table where ruffians and gamblers were gathered around a squat, fur-covered creature that had one of the whirling corkscrews the starbounders-in-training had seen earlier in the creature's right hand. The eight fingers of his left were outstretched on the wood surface before him. A big pile of serendibite was in the center of the table. The creature began stabbing the corkscrew between the gaps in his fingers, increasing the speed until it was just a blur.

As the young Starbounders walked past, Ryic approached the creature and tapped him on the shoulder.

"Do you know where the nearest lang-link is?" Ryic asked.

The distracted alien looked up for just a second, but that's all the time it took for the corkscrew to sever one of his eight fingers. Green fluid oozed from the wound, and some of the onlookers gasped while others reached out to collect their winnings.

Ryic backed away sheepishly. "Sorry," he said. "Carry on."

Before the creature could throttle them, the three

hurried ahead without looking back, pushing through the crowd. They passed by a row of booths where multi-tentacled creatures engaged in what looked like an arm-wrestling tournament, only all their tentacles were being used at the same time. Farther ahead, Zachary spotted a curtained-off booth marked with a picture of a vibrating radio wave above it.

"Over there," he said.

They moved through the crowd and into the booth. A small video screen appeared, displaying a kind of galactic phone book. Among the options were routing numbers to every IPDL base in the outerverse. Zachary reached out and touched the icon for Indigo 8, activating a link to Earth. A single message written in thousands of different languages flashed on the screen. Zachary found the English translation, which read, "Record message now."

Zachary, Ryic, and Kaylee stared ahead at the screen.

"This message is for Henry Madsen. My name is Zachary Night."

"I am Ryic 1,174,831, from the planet Klenarog."

"And this is Kaylee Swanson."

"Our dreadnought crashed on Sirocco, but we survived," said Zachary. "We're contacting you from the Fringg Galaxy Void Market. Please respond as soon as you receive this."

Kaylee gestured toward a send command, and another instruction appeared. The English translation read, "Message sent. Please await response."

The three sat in the closed booth.

"How long will this take?" Zachary asked.

"Lang-link messages sent across the farthest distances of the known outerverse don't take more than ten minutes," Ryic said. "There's an intricate series of probes and satellites that oscillate through folds in space."

Right now Zachary didn't care how it worked. All that mattered was that a plea for help was being sent back home.

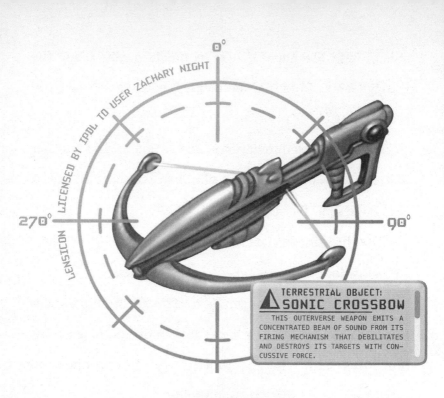

0°

270°

90°

⚠ TERRESTRIAL OBJECT:
SONIC CROSSBOW
THIS OUTERVERSE WEAPON EMITS A
CONCENTRATED BEAM OF SOUND FROM ITS
FIRING MECHANISM THAT DEBILITATES
AND DESTROYS ITS TARGETS WITH CON-
CUSSIVE FORCE.

«NINE»

"I thought you said ten minutes." Zachary sighed.

"Well, this must be old machinery," Ryic said. "Maybe it's still buffering."

"Why don't we call somebody else?" Zachary suggested. "How about someone from your planet?"

"That would be unwise," Ryic said. "The truth is, my people don't know I even went to Indigo 8, and I'd prefer to keep it that way."

"What about those things Skold said?" Zachary asked.

"He only got part of the story right. You see, I wasn't sent away from my planet. I ran away from it."

"Why?" Kaylee asked. "Were people trying to hurt you?"

"No," Ryic said. "They were trying to make me their supreme commander. It was the destiny randomly chosen for me."

Zachary and Kaylee stared at him, confused.

"Leading Klenarogians in battle after battle was not the future I wanted. Instead I departed for the relatively uneventful life of being a Starbounder. Clearly I made a questionable decision."

Before Zachary could express his surprise, the video screen flashed to life, and Henry Madsen appeared before them.

"Starbounders, this is Henry Madsen. If you are viewing this message, remain in the void market. Two IPDL officers are already en route to retrieve you. They should arrive within the hour. You have no idea how happy I am to hear that you're safe."

With that, the message ended. Zachary felt two pairs

of arms wrap around him. He was being hugged from both sides by Ryic and Kaylee.

"Are either of you hungry?" Zachary asked. "Because I suddenly got my appetite back."

"I still have some hard-boiled-egg spaste left," Ryic said.

"I was thinking more like a cheeseburger," Zachary said.

They left the booth and headed for one of the balcony restaurants.

"Maybe I can barter these magnetic tweezers for a meal," Zachary said.

"Or we could just pay for it," Ryic said. "I have a few million serendibite saved up in my galactic bank account."

Zachary and Kaylee looked at him in utter shock.

"What?" Ryic asked. "Did I not mention that before?"

●●●

Zachary and Kaylee sat across from each other at a balcony table dining on greebock steak, the finest cut of space cattle in the outerverse. Ryic had wandered off to get a refill on his drink, but it was taking him an awfully long time to return. As Zachary and Kaylee chewed, they watched a com-bot do battle with a reprogrammed aux-bot in the giant ring. Zachary remembered a completely harmless aux-bot from Indigo 8 that changed the illumination tubes on his SQ's ceiling on his very first day. But this one had its wrench hands replaced with pulverizing hammers and hacksaws.

"And I thought MMA cage matches were brutal," Kaylee said. "This is way cooler."

"You're a little scary sometimes, you know that?" Zachary said.

The com-bot charged, trying to pierce the aux-bot's external rubber shielding with its electrified claws.

"My mother would never approve of this," Kaylee said. "She's a pacifist. We've always been a little different in that regard. She'd drop me off for ballet class, and I'd sneak into the jujitsu dojo next door."

The aux-bot deflected the com-bot's attack, slamming it to the ground. Kaylee jumped up and cheered.

"Finish him!" she shouted.

"Clearly her galactic view hasn't rubbed off on you," Zachary said.

Kaylee sat back down with a smile.

"And your dad?" Zachary asked. "What about him?"

"I wouldn't know. Most of my life he's been off planet. We haven't exactly been close."

Kaylee put her fork down. It looked like she had lost her appetite.

"He's a soulless corporate shill who adds nothing to the outerverse but reinforced steel to space stations. And he's managed to miss all my gymnastics meets while doing it."

"I can see how that might be hard," Zachary said.

Ryic returned to the table without a drink in hand but looking pleased.

"I just met the nicest people," he said. "They were willing to let me into their very exclusive card game even though I didn't know any of the rules. And they said they will keep teaching me until I learn."

"Ryic, was there money involved in this game?" Zachary asked.

"Oh, yes, lots," Ryic said. "And I lost quite a bit of it."

Down below, Zachary spotted two IPDL officers walking the floor. Merchants and outerverse lowlifes watched them suspiciously.

"I think that's our rescue team," Zachary said, pointing.

Kaylee jumped up from the table. "Come on, let's go," she said.

Zachary led the way, descending a spiral staircase back to the main floor. They pushed through the crowd and caught up with the two officers.

"Excuse me," Zachary called out. "I think you're looking for us."

The two officers turned to see the young Starbounders. One was clearly an alien, nine feet tall with braids of hair growing from the back of his neck. The other was an Earthling with a thin mustache. He was slight in stature, especially standing beside his partner.

"I'm Hartwell," the Earthling said. "This is Grino. You must be Zachary."

Zachary nodded. "And this is Ryic and Kaylee."

"We have a buckler waiting in the hangar," Hartwell continued. "Let's get you home."

Hartwell started toward the docking-terminal doors. They hadn't made it past the battle ring when a group of ogre-sized aliens cut them off. They were nearly as tall as Grino but looked much, much meaner.

"The Klenarogian stays with us," one of the ogres said, putting a hand on Ryic's shoulder.

"I'm afraid not," Grino said. "This is official IPDL business. You're going to have to step aside."

None of the ogres budged.

"Maybe I didn't make myself clear," the ogre said. "He's not going anywhere."

His meaty hand tightened its grip on Ryic. Zachary fingered the warp glove in his pocket and eyed the surrounding area for anything he might use as a weapon. But his quick scan came up empty.

Hartwell gave a subtle nod to Grino, who took the ogre's arm in one lightning-fast move and snapped it to the side, dropping him to his knees.

Quickly all the attention on the floor turned to the confrontation. The ogre's cohorts came to his defense, attacking Grino, but the giant IPDL officer kicked the pair of beasts backward. Many aliens hurried into the fray, and still others started to throw down serendibite, as if betting on the outcome of who would win this fight.

The squat, fur-covered creature with eight-fingered hands—well, seven fingers on one hand because of the accident Ryic had caused—lunged at Grino with the spinning corkscrew. Grino thrust out his arm, taking the hit and allowing the whirling blade to jam into his flesh. Grino then ripped the weapon out of his arm and flung it back, impaling the alien's already injured hand.

Outerverse thugs were coming at the group from both sides, and there appeared to be no clear path through them. Even Hartwell seemed at a loss for what to do.

"This way," Zachary called.

He took a turn and leaped over the fence surrounding the battle ring, jumping inside, where the modified aux-bot and com-bot continued to pummel each other. The rest of the group followed, until all five of them were racing across the steel floor of the ring, stepping around the fallen scraps from previous fights. The two bots must have been programmed to attack anything inside the ring, because they were both whizzing toward Zachary. And this was no basement training exercise. One bot's pulverizing hammer was swinging rapidly at his heels. The other's electrified claw was sending arcing bolts from its tip. Just before getting struck, Zachary made a running leap for the fence. His fingers slammed against the metal wire but held fast. He pulled himself ten feet in the air, not feeling the aching in his knuckles until he reached the top. Fortunately the bots couldn't climb. Zachary helped pull Kaylee and Ryic up over the fence, his muscles quivering under their weight. Hartwell and Grino managed on their own.

Once they hit the floor on the other side, they all sprinted for the hangar door. As Hartwell had promised, a buckler waited for them. The ship was about a quarter the size of a dreadnought and shaped like a shield, with three particle guns affixed to the roof. The boarding ramp had already descended, and the five ran into the main cabin, which was filled with all the tools of an outerverse IPDL police craft: shockles, stun balls, and combat sticks.

Zachary, Kaylee, and Ryic were instructed to move quickly to the mechanical webbing and harness themselves in. Hartwell and Grino took their seats in the flight deck and activated the cartograph.

"What if they don't let us out of here?" Zachary called.

"Then I guess we'll find out how effective this ship's particle guns are against hangar shields," Hartwell said.

Grino spoke into the lang-link: "Requesting immediate departure, by order of the Inter-Planetary Defense League."

There was no reply, and the hangar remained sealed shut.

Hartwell swiped his hands across the flight-deck window. Now the display read CHARGING PARTICLE GUNS. Just as the indicator bar reached full, the outer hangar doors began to open.

"Thank you for visiting the Fringg Galaxy Void Market," the robotic voice that had welcomed them echoed. "We hope your stay was pleasant and enjoyable and that you'll come again soon."

The ship took off, exiting through the hangar doors.

"How did you end up in a place like that, anyway?" Hartwell called back into the main cabin.

"Long story," Zachary said.

"We got time," Hartwell replied.

The ship headed into a galactic fold, making its first jump. Once again, Zachary felt his body jostled in every direction, but while it was still an unpleasant sensation, he didn't mind it anymore. Finally, they were going home.

"Might as well get comfortable," Hartwell said. "We

won't hit the next fold for a few hours."

Hartwell and Grino stood up from their flight-deck seats and left the ship's guidance to the internal navigation system. They floated back to the cabin and joined Zachary, Kaylee, and Ryic.

"You three must be starved," Grino said.

"Actually we just ate," Kaylee replied.

"Well, more for me then."

Grino drifted down and cracked open the ship's refrigeration unit. Hartwell hovered right behind him. He pulled out a sonic crossbow and blasted his partner in the back. The force sent Grino face-first to the floor.

Zachary didn't have time to feel shock or horror. He was too busy struggling to free himself from the tethers. So were Ryic and Kaylee. But Hartwell had already turned his weapon on them.

"Nothing personal," Hartwell said. "Somebody wants you dead, and they're willing to pay handsomely for your heads."

Zachary's arms were no longer harnessed, but it didn't matter. Hartwell's crossbow was aimed at his chest. The rogue agent was about to pull the trigger when something flew across Zachary's line of vision. It was Sputnik. Kaylee had pulled the vreek from her pocket and chucked him at Hartwell's face. The space slug dug its teeth into Hartwell's eyes, and Zachary acted fast, activating his warp glove and disarming the traitorous IPDL officer. Kaylee slid out from the tethers and used a set of the ship's shockles to bind Hartwell's ankles to the grating in the floor.

The baby vreek released his grip but kept his teeth bared in case he needed to attack again. "Good job, Sputnik," Kaylee said, stroking her little pet's back.

Zachary pointed the sonic crossbow at Hartwell's forehead, his hands trembling with adrenaline.

"I really dislike these harnesses!" cried Ryic, who continued to try to wrestle himself free. "Couldn't they just put in seat belts?"

∘ ∘ ∘

Hartwell refused to talk. He'd been sitting on the floor with his back against one of the ship's walls for twenty minutes, unable to move. Zachary and Ryic had each taken a turn asking Hartwell who'd hired him. Zachary had used the calm, steely tone he'd seen cops use in action movies. But Hartwell merely smirked in response to every inquiry. Ryic had no better luck.

Now it was Kaylee's turn. She took her questioning in a decidedly more "bad cop" direction, leaning in close to Hartwell's nose, pressing a combat stick against his neck.

"Who put you up to this?" she yelled. "Was it Henry Madsen? Someone at Indigo 8?"

For the first time, Hartwell spoke.

"You're wasting your breath. I never meet the people who hire me. As long as the money transfer clears, I don't ask questions."

"There's something you're not telling us," she said.

"What are you going to do?" Hartwell asked. "Beat it out of me?"

"She's done worse," Ryic said.

Kaylee moved over to Zachary and Ryic and whispered out of Hartwell's earshot.

"This isn't working," she said.

"What options do we have?" Zachary asked. "We can't contact Indigo 8 again. We've already seen how that worked out." He glanced down at Grino's body. Their attempts to revive him had been unsuccessful. "Skold was obviously telling us the truth."

"Why would Director Madsen attempt to have us killed?" Ryic asked.

"I don't know, but don't you find it a little suspicious that we called for help and the next thing you know, someone's here trying to off us?" Kaylee tapped the combat stick against her hand impatiently.

"Hartwell's the only person with information that can lead us to the truth," Zachary said. "We have to find out for certain if it was Madsen or one of his staff members."

"Maybe we can bribe him," Ryic said.

"No," Kaylee said. "We need to be sure that he's not lying."

"How can we guarantee that?" Zachary asked.

"An extractor," Kaylee said.

"That position was outlawed by the IPDL a century ago," Ryic said.

"Well, it didn't stop everyone," Kaylee said. "There are still those who practice the forbidden techniques."

"How do you know?" Zachary asked.

"My father was brought up on charges for doing business with one. Even selling building equipment to an extractor is punishable with ten years in an asteroid prison. But he was exonerated due to a lack of evidence. Still, the name of the extractor he was allegedly involved with always stuck with me. Doveling."

"Where can we find this Doveling?" Zachary asked.

"She was last located on Kibarat, a farming planetoid. We can check the Kepler cartograph to see how to get there."

Zachary and Ryic nodded in agreement. They turned around to see Hartwell sitting as before.

"So, what do you plan on doing with me?" he asked.

"Well, for starters, this," Zachary said.

He grabbed a stun ball off the wall, set it for maximum effect, and threw it at Hartwell's chest. Upon contact, Hartwell was instantly paralyzed. Even his mousy upper lip was frozen in place.

Zachary and Ryic followed Kaylee to the flight deck, where she began setting waypoints to their destination. Zachary had watched carefully as Skold and Wilcox had flown the other ships and, while it was hardly adequate preparation, he thought that together with the week of flight simulation he had experienced on Indigo 8, he could probably figure out his way around the controls.

With their captive immobile in the cabin, they buckled themselves into the flight-deck chairs, and Zachary guided the ship toward the next fold.

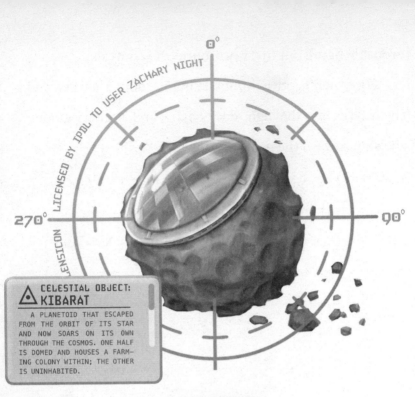

0°

270°

90°

⚠ CELESTIAL OBJECT:
⚠ KIBARAT

A PLANETOID THAT ESCAPED
FROM THE ORBIT OF ITS STAR
AND NOW SOARS ON ITS OWN
THROUGH THE COSMOS. ONE HALF
IS DOMED AND HOUSES A FARM-
ING COLONY WITHIN; THE OTHER
IS UNINHABITED.

«TEN»

"**W**ow," Zachary said.

The sight of Kibarat soaring beside them was breathtaking. The front end of the planetoid had a giant glass dome built over it, with bright green and yellow fields of grass and small farmhouses inside. The back half of the planetoid was uninhabited gray rock, shedding dust particles millions of miles back into the cosmos.

"Hey, Earth to Zachary," Kaylee said. "I asked you a question."

"I'm sorry. What was that?"

"Would you rather lick the floor of a New York City subway car or the armpit of an unshowered stranger?"

They had been passing the time until they reached Kibarat by playing the kinds of games that Zachary remembered from family road trips. Would you rather? was always Danielle's favorite.

"Eww. Gross. Neither," he said.

"Not an option," Ryic said. "You have to pick one."

"And say why," Kaylee added.

"Oh, man, I don't know," Zachary said. "I guess I'd say a stranger's armpit. It's just one person's germs, not thousands'."

"Have you factored in armpit hair and BO?" Kaylee asked.

"I hadn't," Zachary said. "But I am now."

Out the window, they watched as the ship neared an arrival tube on the domed side of the planetoid. Zachary looked over his shoulder to make sure that Hartwell was still incapacitated. He could see by the rigid expression on his face that he was.

The buckler flew into the long clear tube and came out inside the dome. Immediately Zachary realized why Kibarat's fields remained fertile even in the darkest reaches of space. The entire enclosed space radiated heat and light, as brightly as a summer day.

The ship landed in a field of berry shrubs. The engines came to a quiet stop, and after the doors opened, the departure ramp extended to the ground. Zachary, Ryic, and Kaylee armed themselves with sonic crossbows, then exited, leaving Hartwell behind, still stunned and shockled.

"We'll come back for him as soon as we find Doveling," Kaylee said. They reached the bottom of the ramp and Zachary stepped onto the soft grass. He breathed in the air, and the smell of wheat and berries tickled his nostrils. It reminded Zachary very much of home, and that was a comforting feeling. If it weren't for the glass dome high above him, he would have forgotten that they were hurtling through space on a ball of rock.

"Do you know where to find her?" Zachary asked Kaylee.

"No, but these communes are close-knit groups.

Someone should be able to tell us where she is."

There was a farmhouse about a mile away. It seemed like as good a place as any to start.

They walked through a field of tall plants that resembled corn, but their crimson tint exposed them as something not of Earth. Ryic pulled a leaf off one of the stalks and began chewing on it.

"Not as tasty as when the barracks' cook stews them," Ryic said. The leaf was already dyeing his teeth red.

A rustling came from beyond the husks, and a bison-sized beast emerged just a few feet away. Zachary, Kaylee, and Ryic all drew their weapons.

The beast tilted back its huge horned head and let out a trumpeting roar. Zachary put a finger to his ear to try to mute the deafening sound. But there was nothing he could do to avoid getting sprayed by the creature's warm, moist breath.

"We better hope it can't smell what you ate back at Fringg," Ryic said.

"Don't worry, the greebock won't bother you," a friendly voice called out. It belonged to a muscular, olive-skinned alien with four arms who was riding up on a horse with an unusually long body and eight legs. "I saw you fly in. What brings you to Kibarat?"

"Actually, we're looking for someone," Kaylee said. "Goes by the name Doveling. You don't happen to know where we can find her, do you?"

"Of course," the alien replied. "She teaches all of the commune's neophytes out of her stables. If you'd like, I can take you there."

He pointed to the multiple saddles on the horse's back and helped the young Starbounders mount. Zachary had to stretch his legs out extra wide to remain steady atop the rough-furred steed. The alien waited until the three had all settled before giving his horse a swift kick.

"Have you come to study with Doveling?" the alien asked. "Her teachings are wise and inspiring. I can hardly remember what my life was like before my first encounter with her."

A teacher who inspired people? Based on what Kaylee had said, these weren't the characteristics of any extractor Zachary was expecting.

They galloped across the fields, past herds of gree-bocks and several farmhouses. Zachary had gone horseback riding before, but this was much smoother and faster. He looked down and saw a blur of hooves. The clip-clopping was so fast it sounded like a train rattling over wooden tracks.

The horse slowed once they reached a small cluster of stables that made up the center of the space commune. Aliens of all different sizes and colors worked side by side, constructing a new building, with the help of only a few robots.

"This is it," the olive-skinned alien said, stopping the horse before one of the stables. "Perhaps I'll see you again."

Zachary, Kaylee, and Ryic climbed down from the horse.

"Thanks for the ride," Zachary said.

"My pleasure," the alien said. Giving his steed a gentle tap, he departed.

The three approached the stable doors.

"Seems like an odd place to be conducting interrogations," Ryic said.

"These extractors have to blend in," Kaylee said. "Sounds to me as if she's created a perfect cover."

They walked in through the open doors and stood at the back of the stable. Doveling sat cross-legged in a circle with two dozen young aliens, leading them in song. Her pointy ears and delicate features made her look like a fairy without wings.

All Zachary heard was a series of clicks, beeps, and foreign languages, but he could see by the students' smiles and hand-holding that they were probably singing about harmony and togetherness. Once the song was complete, all of the neophytes stood and began leaving the stable.

Zachary, Ryic, and Kaylee walked past them, approaching Doveling.

"Welcome," she said. "Can I help you?"

"Look," Kaylee said, cutting to the chase. "I know what you do."

"I'm sorry?" Doveling asked.

"We don't want to get you in any kind of trouble," Kaylee said. "We just need you to get us some information."

"You must have me confused with someone else. I'm a teacher."

"I know that's not true," Kaylee said. "My father is Liam Swanson. I know all about the high-commission court and the charges brought against him. And although he was exonerated, I know he did business with you."

"Come with me," Doveling said. "We should talk in private."

The stables were empty save for Doveling and a couple of the eight-legged steeds. Still, Doveling led them to one of the old horse stalls and pushed away a pile of hay to reveal a door in the floor. She pulled it open and began to descend a staircase. Kaylee, Zachary, and Ryic followed. Not knowing where this stranger was taking them, Zachary made sure that his finger never hovered far from the trigger of his sonic crossbow.

At the bottom of the steps they entered some kind of underground lab. At its center sat two metal chairs with arm and leg restraints. Lining the shelves were glass jars filled with long, slender needles that looked like the kind used for acupuncture.

"You have it all wrong. He never told you the truth, did he?" Doveling asked.

"What's there to tell? He doesn't care who he sells contracts to as long as he gets his precious promotions," Kaylee replied.

Zachary had seen Kaylee bristly before, but never quite like this.

"Is that what you think?" Doveling shook her head. "Your father was my handler. He was an IPDL agent assigned to utilize my skills in extracting valuable information from outerverse threats."

"No. You're thinking of the wrong guy," Kaylee said. "My dad's a contractor. The only thing he's ever done for the IPDL is get them a good deal on building supplies."

"That's his cover," Doveling said. "Trust me. I've seen him in action. He's the greatest fighter against injustice I have ever met."

"Why would he lie to me?" she asked.

"Perhaps to protect you and to keep you from fearing for his safety every time he leaves you," Doveling said.

Kaylee went quiet. Zachary could see that she was trying to process all Doveling had said about her father.

"So, what kind of information do you need help retrieving?" Doveling pointed to Ryic. "Is it from this one? Because I'll pick his brain clean in an hour, tops."

"What? No!" Ryic cried. "I'm with them."

"Someone wants us dead," Zachary said, jumping in.

"And we'd like you to go into the mind of the man who tried to kill us."

"For a child of Liam, anything," Doveling said. "Bring him to me."

"He's in our ship," Zachary said.

"Go," Doveling said. "I'll get my needles ready."

° ° °

When they returned to the buckler, Zachary and Ryic found Hartwell rummaging through one of the underbins, the effects of the stun ball having worn off. He seemed to be looking for a way to set himself free from the shockles. Zachary used another stun ball to immobilize Hartwell, then he and Ryic carried him to a wheelbarrow, tying a cloth around his eyes and hiding him under some blankets.

They rolled him all the way back to Doveling's stable and carried him down to the secret underground lab. Doveling strapped him into one of the metal chairs, shaved his head bald, and removed the blindfold. Soon he regained his muscular functions.

"Where am I?" Hartwell demanded.

"Relax," Doveling said. "It makes the extraction far quicker."

"This is a violation of my rights!" he shouted.

Zachary was unmoved. "How do you think I felt with your sonic crossbow pointed at my chest?" he said.

Doveling removed a long, thin needle from one of the jars, as fine as a strand of hair, and brought it toward Hartwell's naked skull. She located a precise spot and inserted the tip into his flesh. Though it looked gruesome, Hartwell didn't flinch. He certainly wasn't in pain, and perhaps didn't feel it at all. Doveling extracted the needle and placed it in a new, empty jar.

"What are you doing to me?" Hartwell's temples were beading with sweat.

"Extracting memories," Doveling replied. "There won't be any permanent damage, though."

Hartwell relaxed for the first time.

"Of course, I might rearrange a few things in there," Doveling added. "Do something about those violent tendencies of yours."

She inserted another needle, then removed it. This continued for quite some time, until the empty jar was filled with more than a hundred needles, each with an extracted memory on its tip. It was only after she was finished that Doveling placed a fume mask over Hartwell's nose and mouth, causing him to fall asleep.

"Now the memories need to be read," Doveling said.

Zachary didn't see any microscopes or computers around. In fact, there was no lab equipment of any kind.

"Which one of you wants to be the receptacle?" she asked.

"What?" Zachary exclaimed. "How exactly does this work?"

"I need to insert the needles into one of your frontal lobes. Then the memories will appear in your head as if they were your own."

"You want to stick those needles into our scalps," Ryic said. "Not me. No way."

"Actually, they're slipped into the tiny openings of your tear duct," Doveling said. "With the numbing agent, I've been told it's relatively painless."

"So why don't you do it yourself?" Kaylee asked.

"A surgeon never operates on herself," Doveling said calmly.

Ryic had already made his position known. It would have to be either Zachary or Kaylee, and Kaylee still seemed distracted by the revelations about her dad.

"I'll do it." Zachary was hardly eager but saw no other choice.

"Good. Take a seat."

Zachary sat in the second metal chair. Doveling approached with the jar of needles. She turned to Ryic and Kaylee.

"If you're squeamish, you might want to look away," she said.

Ryic took her up on the warning. Kaylee was less skittish. Doveling took the first of the needles and brought it toward Zachary's face. He flinched at first, but she put a comforting hand on his shoulder. Then with only the slightest pinch, she slipped the needle into the small opening in the corner of his eye. Once it was inserted, Doveling steadily pushed it up and back. The only feeling Zachary could relate it to was the time he got stitches in his knee after it had been numbed. It was like a gentle, disconcerting tug on his eyeball.

"The best place to read a memory is just above the ocular nerve," Doveling said.

Suddenly an image flooded Zachary's brain. It showed

Hartwell as a boy swimming in a pool. It was as vivid as if Zachary had experienced it himself. "Honey," a motherly voice called. "Come dry off. It's time for lunch."

Doveling pulled out the needle. It felt to Zachary like a splinter being removed.

"How recent was the memory?" she asked.

"That one was from his childhood," Zachary said.

"Okay, let's try one of these," Doveling said. "It's trial and error."

As the next needle went in, Zachary got a flash of a violent scene. He was watching Hartwell's father pour gasoline around a man tied to a chair. He struck a match and was about to let it drop.

"I've seen enough of that one," Zachary said.

Doveling removed the needle. And so began a process of, one by one, inserting the obscure and often disturbing memories of Hartwell's past. The collection of thoughts, images, and conversations quickly painted a picture of this traitorous assassin, who had learned everything he needed to know about being a ruthless mercenary from his father.

She was about halfway through the jar when Zachary

experienced a memory of interest. In it Hartwell was receiving a holo-mail on his phone, and though the sender was unknown, the message was clear: "Starbounders targeted for termination." Pictures of Zachary, Kaylee, and Ryic followed. "Last confirmed location: Fringg Galaxy Void Market." An image appeared of the giant space station, shrouded in darkness. "Once complete, proceed to Tenretni and terminate the cyber hack called Quee. No visual facial ID available." A picture appeared of a human hand typing with four neon tattoos inked across the knuckles. The rest of the body was obscured in dark shadows. "Last confirmed location: Discrape Towers." A final image appeared of an abandoned building with indecipherable symbols drawn on the marquee outside.

"Quick, hand me a pen," Zachary said. "And something to write on."

Doveling removed the needle from his tear duct, then fetched him a pencil and a piece of paper. Zachary transcribed the sign he had seen in his head as best he could.

"Hartwell was telling the truth. He doesn't know who hired him to kill us. But whoever it was employed him to kill someone else, too. A cyber hack named Quee living in the Tenretni District. This is the name of the building she was last seen in."

"Then we'll go to Tenretni," Kaylee said. "What other leads do we have?"

"That city is located beyond the Asteroid Curtain," Doveling said. "Past what felons call the Indigo Divide. Once you enter those far reaches of space, there are no lang-link probes. No life lines to the IPDL."

"Can I open my eyes yet?" Ryic asked. He still had his back turned and his hands covering his face.

"Yes, it's fine, Ryic," Kaylee said. "We got what we need."

"What would you like us to do with him?" Zachary asked, gesturing to the unconscious Hartwell.

"Once I finish remapping his neurons, I'll put him to work in the fields," Doveling said. "He'll be happy here. They usually are."

"What do you mean?" Zachary asked.

"The criminals I extract from all end up making Kibarat their home," Doveling said. "That alien who brought you to me—he used to have blood on his hands. Now it's just dirt. And while some view remapping as inhumane, I have no doubt it gives them a better life than one in prison, behind bars and in shockles."

Doveling led them up the staircase and into the stable. As they emerged inside the empty stall, Doveling brushed the pile of hay back over the trapdoor. Then they walked toward the exit.

"Should you ever need to seek refuge again, you're always welcome here," Doveling said.

A new group of young aliens was already forming a semicircle in the center of the stable, sitting cross-legged and holding writing tablets in their laps.

"I have another class to teach," Doveling said. "Today we're learning about the Three Virtues of the Lamasori. It was he who said, 'Truth has many curtains. But one need not pull back all of them to see the light.'"

With that, Zachary, Kaylee, and Ryic departed. Upon stepping out into the warm glow of Kibarat's dome, Zachary viewed the workers tilling the fields differently. It was impossible to tell which ones were peaceful pilgrims who had come here to seek a simpler way of life and which had been reprogrammed to think that was what they'd desired.

The distance to the buckler felt longer on foot than it did by horseback. Kaylee was still lost in thought.

"I know what you learned about your father must be confusing," Zachary said.

"It is," Kaylee replied. "All this time, I thought he was away from us for some stupid job. But now I find out that everything he sacrificed was so he could help make this outerverse a better place."

"Sounds like you two aren't so different after all," Zachary said.

A smile started to form on her face. "I'm guessing all those cuts on his hands weren't from filing papers."

They reached the buckler just as the dome's daylight simulation was beginning to cycle to night. They ascended the boarding ramp and returned to their seats in the ship's flight deck. This time, Ryic inputted the waypoints to Tenretni on the planet Irafas, charting their course on the Kepler cartograph.

"What I still can't understand is how a cyber hack in Tenretni has anything to do with someone wanting us dead," Kaylee said.

"Maybe there's been a flaw in our logic," Ryic said. "All

this time we've been assuming that a person from Indigo 8 is behind this. What if it's not a person?"

"Now you've lost me," Zachary said.

"Think about it," Ryic said. "The glitch in the Qube. The malfunctioning stun ball during the Chameleon game. The unlocked terrarium. The sabotaged starbox. They're all things that Cerebella could have done."

"You're saying Indigo 8's mainframe computer wants us dead?" Zachary asked. "Why?"

"I don't know," Ryic said, "but she would have received the transmission we sent from the void market. She could have hired Hartwell to kill us. As for Quee, perhaps the hacker stumbled onto the truth. Who better to uncover Cerebella's plot?"

Zachary had to admit it was a compelling case.

"Computers have taken on a life of their own before," Kaylee said. "Haven't you ever read about the Binary Colonies?"

If it was Cerebella who was responsible for all of this, they were up against a more powerful adversary than they'd even thought possible.

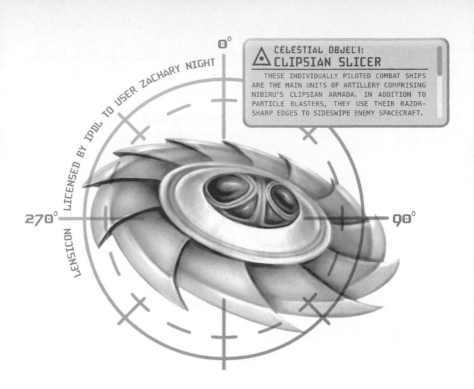

LENSICON

0°

270°

90°

CELESTIAL OBJECT:
CLIPSIAN SLICER

THESE INDIVIDUALLY PILOTED COMBAT SHIPS
ARE THE MAIN UNITS OF ARTILLERY COMPRISING
NIBIRU'S CLIPSIAN ARMADA. IN ADDITION TO
PARTICLE BLASTERS, THEY USE THEIR RAZOR-
SHARP EDGES TO SIDESWIPE ENEMY SPACECRAFT.

«ELEVEN»

Zachary made gentle sweeping motions with his hands, guiding the buckler through a calm expanse of space. The young Starbounders had deactivated the autopilot so they could all get some practice in. It also helped pass the time during the long flight between space folds. Kaylee and Ryic were in the main cabin playing an impromptu game of zero-gravity soccer. Kaylee had blown air into a rubber glove taken from one of the first aid kits and was kicking it from wall to wall as Ryic tried to intercept it.

"Come on, Ryic, if you're frustrated, talk some trash," Kaylee said.

"I have no interest in speaking about garbage," he replied. "My focus is on winning."

Zachary could hear Kaylee kick the makeshift balloon ball. There was a pop followed by a whizzing sound, and the deflated glove zipped past his shoulder, making a high-pitched squeal before smacking into the cockpit window. Kaylee soared up beside him.

"Sorry, hit the tip of my boot," she said.

"That sound," Zachary said, still cringing. "It's worse than nails on a chalkboard for me."

"Really?" Kaylee asked. "A deflating balloon?"

"Yep, ever since I was little. My parents hired a clown to make balloon animals at my first-grade birthday party. I hid in my bedroom the whole time."

"That's so sad," Kaylee said, suppressing a laugh. "Then again, the sound of an emery board is like a knife jabbing at my eardrum. That's why my fingers look like they're in desperate need of a manicure. Which you couldn't pay me to get, by the way."

"Your hands do resemble those of a hairless ichtyo-pod," Ryic said.

"That better be a compliment, or you're about to see these hands close up," Kaylee said, making two fists.

"It is a smooth-skinned, glorious creature," Ryic said, clearly lying, "renowned for its beauty."

But Zachary wasn't listening anymore. His focus had turned to a cloud of gray that stretched as far as he could see. "What is that?"

As the ship got closer to it, it became apparent that the cloud was made up of millions of rocks banging into each other, shattering into smaller pieces.

"The Asteroid Curtain," Ryic said. "Past there, we're on our own."

"I think we already are," Zachary said.

"Some say it was caused by the big bang itself," Ryic said. "That everything beyond it is part of the outerverse that predates existence as we know it."

"Maybe it's time to put the autopilot back on," Zachary said.

With a gesture, he disengaged the manual command

of the buckler. The ship continued on its course, and the closer they came to the Curtain, the better Zachary felt about his decision to relinquish control. He could have dodged the larger chunks of rock with his own steering, but there were tiny ones, too, so small that they went undetected until the ship nearly made impact with them.

The autopilot's collision-avoidance system was working overtime. As the buckler wove through the maze of hurtling rocks, Zachary, Ryic, and Kaylee were treated to a roller-coaster ride. It was like Six Flags but without the tracks. If he hadn't been strapped in, Zachary would have been turned into a human pinball. As soon as they crossed to the other side of the Asteroid Curtain, the ship started beeping and a flashing red message appeared on the cockpit window: **WARNING: EXITING REGISTERED IPDL TERRITORY. OUTERVERSE DATABASE LIMITED FROM THIS POINT ON. HIGHLY CAUTION AGAINST CONTINUING.**

Zachary eyed the Kepler cartograph and saw that while previously the space field had been extensively labeled, it was now filled with countless unidentified dots signifying yet-to-be-explored planets and unvisited moons. Only the most populated destinations were marked on the map. Fortunately, one of them was Tenretni.

The ship headed for the nearest fold. Like space veterans, Zachary, Ryic, and Kaylee braced themselves for the jump, but instead of finding empty space on the other side, they were engulfed by hundreds of strange white disc-like ships.

Zachary saw manned cockpits at the center of each of them, and a ring of blades around their perimeter. The crosshairs of his lensicon honed in on one of the ships, and he blinked twice.

⚠ CELESTIAL OBJECT:
CLIPSIAN SLICER

THESE INDIVIDUALLY PILOTED COMBAT SHIPS ARE THE MAIN UNITS OF ARTILLERY COMPRISING NIBIRU'S CLIPSIAN ARMADA. IN ADDITION TO PARTICLE BLASTERS, THEY USE THEIR RAZOR-SHARP EDGES TO SIDESWIPE ENEMY SPACECRAFT.

THEY SHOULD BE TREATED AS HOSTILE.

"This can't be good," Zachary said.

"Thank you, Captain Obvious," Kaylee replied.

"Initiate camouflage shield," Ryic said.

On Ryic's voice command, a cool blue tint filled the ship, indicating that the buckler's cloaking mechanism had been activated. If their sudden arrival had been spotted by any of the slicers, at least they couldn't be seen now.

"We should turn around and go back through the fold," Ryic said.

Zachary glanced at the cartograph.

"There's only one more bound to Tenretni," he said. "And I don't see any other way to get there."

"Yes, but navigating through Nibiru's armada is too risky," Ryic replied. "What if they have distortion sensors? It would expose our optical camouflage and we'd be space dust."

"The slower we move, the fewer gravity ripples we'll make," Kaylee said. "We should be able to glide by undetected."

Zachary gestured in front of the holographic display, turning off the autopilot and resuming manual control of the ship. He reduced the buckler's speed to a cosmic crawl and they passed unnoticed through a cluster of idling slicers. As they got particularly close to one, Zachary was able to get a view of the metallic blades jutting out from the ghostly discs. Each disc had sharpened teeth like a saw, with scraps of other ships still stuck between the blades. He could also see the Clipsian pilot sitting inside, motionless, as if waiting for a command from one of the scouting beacons blinking brightly against the darkness of space. Suddenly, one of the beacons above them began to move down, and a fleet of a dozen slicers followed it. They were heading right for the buckler.

"I knew it," Ryic said. "We've been caught. You two never listen to me! Now we're all goners. We're done for."

But the beacon and the trail of ships behind it flew past their invisible buckler, continuing along on what must have been a routine training exercise, making sharp ninety-degree turns and quick one-eighties.

Zachary and Kaylee turned to Ryic. He shrugged.

"So maybe I overreacted a little," he said.

The buckler continued past the armada's smaller ships, toward larger and more ominous ones that Zachary's lens-icon identified as urchins. They had large spikes protruding from their circular bodies. Making them even more deadly were their magnetic hulls, which would draw any nearby craft into the reach of the spikes.

"My guess is they're planning another attack," Kaylee said. "Probably on some defenseless planet. They only ever strike the weak and unarmed."

Zachary hated the thought of another innocent planet joining the Ulam's Outerverse Memorial.

"What a bunch of cowards," Zachary said. "I'd like to see them stand up against the IPDL. A fleet that could punch them back."

"They never will," Kaylee replied. "Professor Olari says that Nibiru only goes into battles he knows he can win."

Just then the ship thudded against something. Zachary looked out the cockpit window to see what they had collided with. But when he peered into space, he saw nothing.

"I felt it, too," said Ryic. "I'll go check the other portholes."

Ryic unbuckled himself from the flight deck-chair and floated to the main cabin. Zachary and Kaylee remained seated, doing a quick systems analysis. They didn't find anything unusual.

"Guys," Ryic called. "I think I found our problem. It

looks like we hooked one of those scouting beacons in our tailfin."

Zachary peered into the corner of the front window, where a holographic projection displayed a view of the back of the ship. He could see the flashing from the light that had become tangled around one of the ship's steering flaps.

"If we don't get that thing off quick, we're going to become slicer feed," Kaylee said.

Zachary steered the ship so that it made quick jolts, accelerating and decelerating. He thought he could make the beacon break free.

"It's still stuck," Ryic shouted. "Try something else."

"Better yet, let me," Kaylee said, tightening her seat belt.

She waved her arms and took control of the ship's steering mechanism, twisting her hands so the buckler would do a barrel roll, first clockwise, then counterclockwise.

"How about now?" Kaylee asked.

"Nope," Ryic said, holding on tight. "And we've got bigger problems. About twenty slicers are following us."

"Do they look like they're getting ready to attack?" Zachary asked.

"No," Ryic said.

"Then chances are they don't even realize we're here. They probably think this is just another routine training exercise. If we stay the course, we can make it to the next fold and they'll be none the wiser."

"They're going to grow suspicious if we continue flying in a straight line," Kaylee said, her face glowing in the blue light. "Didn't you see them earlier? The beacon was making sharp turns and about-faces. We better do the same."

Zachary remembered the maneuvers he'd just seen, and tried to replicate them as best he could, first commanding the buckler to tip ninety degrees upward, then to make a wide turn to the right.

"So far, so good," Ryic called.

Looking at the rearview projector, Zachary could see that the fleet of slicers was copying the buckler's every move as he continued to simulate the precision drills. The plan seemed to be working perfectly. Despite the zigging and zagging, they were still making steady progress in the direction of the next space fold.

"The beacon!" Ryic exclaimed. "It's finally come loose."

"That's great," Kaylee said. "If we can shake it off, the

Clipsians will follow it instead of us."

Zachary made another tight turn, only this time there was a loud clang at the back of the ship, followed by an explosion.

"Ryic, what happened?" Zachary wished he could be in two places at once.

"The beacon just got sucked up into our influx tube."

Almost instantly, a message appeared on the holographic display. CAMOUFLAGE SHIELD COMPROMISED. ENEMY DISTORTION SENSORS HAVE IDENTIFIED SHIP.

The cool blue glow inside the buckler was now gone. Surely they were visible to their adversaries, naked and exposed. Ryic had floated back to the flight deck and buckled himself in beside Zachary and Kaylee.

"We need to bound out of here, and quick," he said.

Zachary was trying to move the ship as fast as it would go, charting a straight shot toward the next fold. According to the cartograph, it was still a fair distance away. A particle blast fired across the top of the buckler, narrowly missing them.

"If you don't get a little more creative with your flying,

we're easy targets out here," Kaylee said.

"I'm trying to get us to that space fold as fast I can," Zachary replied, thrusting his hand forward.

Just then they heard an earsplitting screech. The awful sound had come from one of the slicers' outer blades thrashing the buckler's exterior. Impact from the collision sent them spinning. Zachary tried to wrestle control of the ship, but it tumbled off course. Zachary glanced back to see that the side of the buckler had been dented inward like a squeezed tin can.

Before he could get on a straight trajectory, the ship was struck again, this time in the back end of the spacecraft.

Then the hum inside the buckler became very quiet.

"We just lost power to the engines," Zachary said.

Kaylee went to the cabin to assess the damage from the last blow.

"We won't be able to repair this from the inside," she called to the flight deck.

The slicers were circling back for another attack.

"How are we supposed to make it to the next fold without our engines?" Ryic asked.

"Our forward momentum will get us there," Zachary assured him.

"But not if those slicers do first," Kaylee said. "We need more speed."

"If those slicer blades keep poking at us, this ship is going to pop like that rubber glove," Ryic said. He was pointing at the deflated glove still sticking to the cockpit window.

"Ryic, that's it," Zachary said.

"Why do you sound so excited?" Ryic asked. "I see very few positives to such an unforgiving end."

"No, the rubber glove. It gave me an idea."

Particle blasts were coming in, bouncing off the buckler's sides.

"How do the engines on this ship operate?" Zachary asked.

"By expelling superheated matter and gas at extraordinary speeds," Kaylee answered.

"Okay, what if we applied the same principle, only instead we used oxygen to propel us forward," Zachary said. "The oxygen that's inside this ship."

"That's crazy," Kaylee said. "You want to pop our ship

like a balloon and use the air we're breathing to push us forward?"

"You clearly misunderstood me," Ryic added. "I was saying that it's a bad thing."

"It's a fine idea in theory," Kaylee said. "But even if we did make it through the fold, we might suffocate first."

"Very, very bad," Ryic said.

"The ship's bio regulators will keep us alive until we get to Tenretni," Zachary said. Even if Ryic and Kaylee didn't seem entirely sold, Zachary was already putting his plan into action. "Ryic, take over for me. Kaylee, grab each of us one of those regulators."

"What are you going to do?" Ryic asked.

"Pop this balloon."

Zachary pulled a photon cannon from the overhead bin.

Two slicers seemed to cut into the buckler at the same time, slamming it from both sides. Without the engines to power them, they were sitting ducks.

Kaylee returned to Zachary, empty-handed.

"All the bio regulators have been sabotaged," she said.

"How is that possible?" Zachary asked.

"That's what he was doing!" Ryic called out.

"What who was doing?" Kaylee snapped back.

"Hartwell. When Zachary and I came back to retrieve him, he was awake," Ryic said. "The stun ball had partially worn off, and I found him rummaging through some of the underbins. It looked to me like he was searching for a way to free himself. But it turns out he was within arm's reach of the regulators, tampering with them."

"Now what?" Kaylee asked.

"Get back in the flight deck, buckle in tight, and hold your breath," Zachary said, moving to the rear of the cabin. He grabbed the equipment rack with one hand and aimed his photon cannon squarely at the back end of the buckler. Then Zachary fired. And fired. And fired again.

On the third blast the photon cannon blew a grapefruit-sized hole in the cabin wall. With explosive force, oxygen was sucked out of the hole, launching the buckler forward with a burst of acceleration. Zachary felt like his skin was going to be ripped from his body. Only this was a thousand times stronger. Hand over hand, he pulled himself along the equipment racks back to the flight deck. Ryic and Kaylee were staring straight ahead.

Through the cockpit window he could see that Kaylee was gunning toward the space fold. The slicers were now struggling to catch up, trying to intercept them before they bounded away. Zachary pushed off the equipment rack to vault himself down to a seat of his own, but in the process he knocked a stun ball from one of the belts hanging on the wall. As soon as it went airborne, it was sucked backward, rocketing through the main cabin and lodging itself in the hole that Zachary had just blown in the wall.

The stun ball completely blocked the airflow, cutting off the buckler's propulsion. And while it gave them a moment to catch their breath, the decrease in acceleration allowed the slicers to close the gap.

"I can't reach," Ryic said after stretching his arm back to the very limits of his unearthly ability.

Kaylee had a different idea. She used her warp glove to try to tug the ball away. But it would take more weight and strength than she had in one hand alone.

Zachary had already launched himself from the seat and was on his way to remove the obstruction blocking the hole. He tried to pull it free, but the stun ball held fast. It occurred to him that he might have a better chance of pushing it through. Zachary anchored himself against the wall and began pounding his boot against the sphere. He was getting winded fast, the air having thinned significantly.

With each successive kick, the stun ball wedged itself tighter into the hole. He had exhausted every ounce of might in his legs, yet the ball refused to give. Zachary was beginning to see stars, and not the ones outside the ship's rear porthole window. His blurry vision fell on a mag mop snapped onto the wall. If he couldn't boot the ball through, maybe he could bat it out.

Zachary reached out and grabbed the mop. He choked up on the handle and took a mighty swing, keeping his eye on the ball just like his dad had taught him to do during one of their many baseball practices in the backyard.

The mesh and metal end struck the stun ball with tremendous force and knocked it clear out of the ship. Instantly the oxygen went whooshing out of the buckler once more, and Zachary felt the results of it immediately, both the ship surging forward and losing his breath. Once again he used the equipment rack and tried to pull himself back to safety.

"You did it before," Kaylee called. "Come on, you can make it!"

Zachary wanted to respond, but his mouth couldn't form the words. He struggled to keep his eyes open as the ship zoomed toward the space fold. Suddenly Ryic's outstretched arm grabbed him firmly and pulled him back to the flight deck, where the air was richer and more breathable. But it was in vain.

Just as the ship starbounded, Zachary passed out.

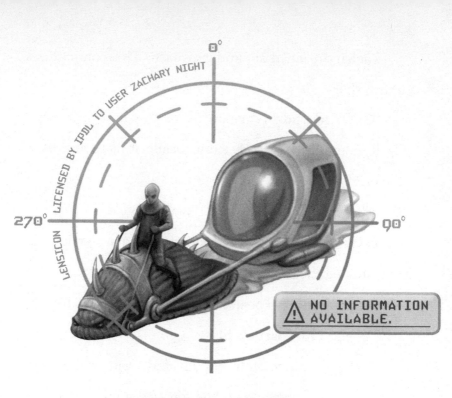

0°

270°

90°

⚠ NO INFORMATION AVAILABLE.

«TWELVE»

Zachary's eyes opened. A blinding light reflected through the flight-deck window. It took a moment to gather his senses. Ryic and Kaylee were passed out in their seats, but he could see they were breathing. The buckler had touched down on a massive landing strip, just one spacecraft among hundreds. From their spot at the edge of the lot, they were just a short walk from a row of small, pointy buildings that were sticking out of a rolling fog.

Zachary reached out and gave each of his companions a firm shake.

"Guys," he said. "Wake up."

Ryic and Kaylee slowly came to, adjusting their eyes to the brightness.

"We're safe," Zachary said. "We've landed."

Releasing his safety belt, Ryic touched a purple ooze that stained the midsection of his shirt.

"I . . . I think I've been hit," he said, alarmed. "It must have been a stray particle blast."

Zachary immediately got up and went to his side. Kaylee looked less worried. She scooped some of the ooze up with her finger and examined it more closely. Then she licked it.

"Ah, you're a cannibal!" Ryic exclaimed. "I knew it."

"Unless you bleed peanut-butter-and-jelly spaste, I think you'll survive," Kaylee said.

Ryic stood up and pulled a punctured pouch out from his clothing.

"I didn't realize I had that in there," he said.

Zachary was equal parts relieved and frustrated.

"Come on," he said. "Tenretni awaits."

The three climbed down the buckler's departure ramp onto a slick black sidewalk much like the ones at Indigo 8. Arrows directed them toward one of the small buildings at the edge of the lot. Passengers from other arriving ships joined them on the sidewalk. Others passed in the opposite direction, ready to head back into space.

As they got closer to the edge of the lot, Zachary realized that these weren't small buildings at all, but the very tops of skyscrapers. Looking down, he could see that the entire landing lot had been built thousands of feet above the surface of the planet. The rolling fog was actually clouds.

Zachary, Ryic, and Kaylee entered the top floor of one of the skyscrapers and found themselves inside a circular glass elevator along with a dozen other arriving visitors. Once the doors closed, the elevator rapidly descended, going below the clouds and revealing the dense city of Tenretni.

It was a sprawling metropolis, with multiple tiers of development. Sidewalks, roads, and buildings were stacked layer upon layer, all supported the same way as the landing lot: on giant girders. The elevator came to its first stop on the 170th floor, which was the entry point for the highest tier of the city. The best dressed of the newly arriving travelers disembarked.

Zachary tapped one of the elevator passengers about to exit on the shoulder and showed her the scrap of paper with the symbols he'd drawn.

"Excuse me," he said. "Do we need to get off here to get to this building? Discrape Towers?"

The passenger laughed.

"Bottom tier," she said in a deep voice.

The elevator resumed its descent, not stopping again until it reached the eighty-fifth floor. This led to Tenretni's second-level district. Now the moderately attired visitors departed. That left only Zachary, Ryic, Kaylee, and three others, whose filthy appearance made it obvious that none of them belonged to the privileged class.

One, a hunched, wrinkled humanoid figure with stringy hair and fungus growing from her arms, stared at Zachary. Then without warning she grabbed Zachary's hand with her bony fingers. Before he could pull free, she stuck out her long tongue and drew it along his palm, past his wrist and toward his elbow. She snapped it back into her mouth and let out a cackle.

"Pay me and I'll tell you your future," she said. "At least what's left of it."

The elevator reached the first floor and Zachary quickly exited.

"Don't you want to know the death and misery I tasted on you?" asked the crone, hobbling after him.

"Take your crazy someplace else," Kaylee said.

Zachary was still wiping the spittle from his arm as his friends came up beside him. Looking around, they found themselves below so many roads and passageways that it was hard to believe they weren't underground. The densely populated lower tier looked to Zachary like it had once been a place of great prosperity. Perhaps it was over-population or overcrowding that had led to its demise. Either way, its infrastructure was crumbling, and any investment in the future of Tenretni had been directed upward, not down here. Where above they had spotted automated hover-cars zipping around crystal pathways, on the bottom tier rickshaws were pulled by enormous slithering alien creatures who left trails of slime pooling in the roads.

Zachary broke out coughing as his nostrils filled

with an unpleasant odor. The air had a smoggy brownish hue, and Kaylee was trying to wave it away from her face. Ryic was the only one who seemed unfazed. All the pollution in Tenretni had seemed to settle down here on the ground, leaving the levels above pristine and clear. Zachary lifted his shirt up over his nose and took a breath, turning to a once-majestic building sitting at the center of a park whose grass had all dried up, overrun with weeds and dirt. His lensicon targeted the building and he blinked twice.

NO INFORMATION AVAILABLE.

Zachary turned to an old, run-down bank on the street corner. The same message appeared. Then his eyes spun to a floating car moving overhead. *No information.* A strange alien passed them by. Still nothing.

"Looks like we won't be getting much help from our lensicons," Zachary said, feeling more than ever the direness of their search.

The search for Discrape Towers was even harder because they were unable to read the native language.

Finding the signage from Hartwell's extracted memory seemed impossible.

One of the rickshaws came around the corner, and the alien manning the reins pulled it to a stop alongside some pedestrians, who climbed aboard.

"Maybe we can hitch ourselves a ride," Kaylee said.

They waited until another of the two-wheeled passenger carts rolled up, and Zachary ran out to stop it. The creature slowed.

"Can you take us to Discrape Towers?" Zachary asked the alien driver.

The driver shrugged, not understanding. Zachary reached out to show him the piece of paper. The alien looked at the drawing and shook his head as if he couldn't read it either. Then he tapped the side of the spiked beast hauling the wagon. The beast turned, looked at the paper, and nodded. Clearly, the driver wasn't the brains of this operation. He gestured for Zachary, Ryic, and Kaylee to get in, and the three sat upon the torn satin cushions of the rickshaw. Burning sticks of incense were wedged precariously in the cracks of the wooden frame of the carriage, sending up smoke that filled the wagon with the smell of tangerines and roses, a welcome break from the stink outside.

The beast pulled them forward, more swiftly than any seven-hundred-pound blob should have been able to travel. They passed alleys filled with trash and discovered where it all came from. Long tubes ejected it in sudden bursts from the tiers above. Stranger still was an orderly line of residents waiting for their turn to pick through the fresh scraps.

While they were still moving, the driver extended an open palm toward Zachary and let it linger there.

"Looks like he wants us to pay him," Kaylee said.

"Do you think he'll accept my galactic bank account number?" Ryic asked.

"Not likely," Kaylee said.

"Well, then I hope this is sufficient," Ryic said, pulling a cube of serendibite from his pocket and offering it to the driver. "Enough?" he asked, enunciating the word slowly.

The alien looked at it and his eyes lit up big and wide. He let out an exclamation in his alien tongue and began weeping.

"Oh, no, I've upset him," Ryic said.

"I'm pretty sure those are tears of joy," Kaylee said. "I'm guessing that's more money than he's ever seen in his life."

They continued on, passing marble statues aged beyond recognition, reminders of the once-thriving city that previously existed on the ground level. The enormous blob slowed, coming to a stop before a hotel. It was the very building that Zachary had seen in Hartwell's memory. There above the door were the same symbols he'd quickly transcribed on the paper.

The driver ran around and opened the rickshaw's rear doors. He lent an overeager hand to Zachary, Ryic, and Kaylee, helping each of them down to the ground. Then he pulled off his overcoat and laid it over a pool of slime on the sidewalk so the three wouldn't have to get their shoes dirty. They nodded appreciatively as they stepped across his jacket.

"During the extraction, I saw something else," Zachary said as they approached the entrance to the hotel. "Quee's knuckles had neon tattoos on them. Small grids with colored squares. Keep an eye out."

They walked through a broken revolving door. The glass panes had been shattered, and all that remained was the rusty metal frame. Their entrance did not go unnoticed by the two dozen cyber hacks sitting on dirty couches inside. Heads turned, looking up from their palm and wrist tablets. Any one of them could have been Quee. And Zachary was wondering what the best strategy was for finding him. Perhaps an inconspicuous survey of all the hackers' knuckles? Or delicate one-on-ones in which Quee's name was only brought up after trust had been earned? Maybe they would quietly—

"Are any of you here named Quee?" Ryic shouted to the room. "We're looking for a cyber hack by the name of Quee."

A handful of the squatters immediately scattered, hopping out of windows and slipping through cracks in the wall. So much for Zachary's plan.

"We're not here to get any of you in trouble," Zachary called. "We've actually come to warn Quee about some danger he's in."

A female lizard-like alien emerged from beneath a table where she'd set up a patchwork of computer screens. The creature was about the size of Zachary's sister, Danielle, but covered in scales. She had long, bony fingers, three on each hand.

"Quee's not here," the alien said. "But I can lead you to him."

"How do we know we can trust you?" Kaylee asked.

"Who said anything about trusting me?" the alien replied. "This is bottom-tier Tenretni. If you're looking for loyalty, try the eighty-fifth floor or higher."

The alien moved toward the entrance to a stairwell and glanced back before continuing on.

"Well?" she asked.

Zachary, Ryic, and Kaylee decided to follow. What choice did they have? They headed downward, descending even lower into what appeared to be the basement of the old hotel. There they saw a hole in the wall that had a tangle of colored wires running out of it. It looked like dynamite had blasted through thick layers of concrete to form the opening. The creature crawled through, leading them into a tunnel. Inside, Zachary was struck by an impressive sea of giant rubber tubing that stretched for miles.

"All of the power and information for the city above runs through here," said the alien. "It took us years to tunnel in, but now we siphon power and information from the grid."

"If you don't trust us, then why are you telling us this?" Zachary asked.

"Because if you're here for the reason you claim to be, you won't be getting out of here alive," the alien said.

They continued through the underground corridor, occasionally passing more spots where the power cables had been tampered with. The alien stopped at a side door.

"Quee resides through here," the creature said. "Follow me."

They entered to find a room roughly the size of a school classroom. It had been converted into secret living quarters and a work station, filled with both home furnishings and computers, all of which looked like they had been scavenged from the trash heaps. A hooded figure sat in the far corner of the room with its back turned to them.

"Quee, you have visitors," the alien said.

The figure turned to reveal a humanoid with large fish eyes on the sides of his head and a thick snout. As his gloved fingers typed on a flexible keyboard resting on his lap, a voice echoed out from a pair of speakers connected to it.

"What do you want with me?" the computerized voice asked.

"An IPDL officer turned mercenary was hired to kill us," Zachary said. "Once he was finished, you were next on his list. Any idea who might want you dead?"

"I have my fair share of enemies," the voice replied. "Before we continue, I'll need to verify that what you're saying is true." Quee gestured to a monitor with electrodes attached to it. "Standard lie detector test."

"You don't have to stick anything into my eyeballs, do you?" Zachary asked.

"No," Quee answered.

"Then I'm fine with it."

Zachary walked over and took a seat next to the monitor. Quee removed his gloves to pull off the paper backings covering the adhesive side of the electrodes. Zachary's eyes peered down at the alien's knuckles and he was shocked to see that Quee didn't have any tattoos on them.

Zachary immediately jumped to his feet. He drew his sonic crossbow and took aim.

"Who are you?" Zachary demanded. "I know you're not Quee."

The fish-eyed humanoid snatched a photon gun from under the table and pointed it at Zachary. With his free hand, he typed into the keyboard.

"What now?" the voice asked.

The lizard-like alien who had led them here stepped forward.

"I'm Quee," she said.

Zachary looked at her with a smirk. "I don't think so. Try again."

"I'll hook myself up to that machine if you don't believe me."

"I saw an image of Quee's hands," Zachary said. "They were more human than yours. And the knuckles had neon tattoos on them."

Now it was Quee who was smirking. "Don't you think I know where every surveillance camera on this planet is located? That's why I never use my real hands when I'm hacking." She walked over to an old mahogany dresser and slid open a drawer. It was filled with pairs of robotic hands, some humanoid, some alien. One of the humanoid pairs had the same tattoos that Zachary had spied in Hartwell's memory. "All taken from discarded carapaces."

Zachary lowered the sonic crossbow. Quee signaled for the humanoid to do the same with the gun.

"Every precaution has to be taken in my line of work," Quee said. "Now what else can you tell me about this mercenary?"

Zachary recounted every last detail he could remember about Hartwell. Quee listened closely before speaking again.

"I took a job recently, one that paid extraordinarily well. Not your typical identity theft or data trolling. I was contracted to create a computer virus that would be able to activate the emergency defenses of any security system, even if no imminent threat was present. Typically cyber hacks are hired to *de*activate security systems. It felt funny from the start, but I never ask questions. Professional courtesy."

"Why would Cerebella need a hacker to make a computer virus?" Ryic asked Kaylee and Zachary.

Zachary was thinking the same thing. This changed their theory completely.

"Who would be looking to do something like that?" Kaylee asked.

"I don't know," Quee said. "But there might be a way to find out. It won't be easy though. We'll have to go to the galactic bank where my payment was wired. The only way I can hack into their mainframe is to hard-line it on-site. Most of my employers cover their tracks, but any track can be uncovered, assuming you have the right tools."

Quee held up a pair of five-fingered robotic hands.

"These look like good ones," she said.

"Slight problem," Zachary said. "Our ship was damaged on the way here. We'll need to repair it before we leave."

"Lucky for you, I know a few people who might be able to help," Quee said.

° ° °

Zachary, Ryic, and Kaylee stood on the landing lot watching with Quee as a grease-stained alien welded a metal plate over the hole at the back of the buckler.

"That doesn't look very secure," Ryic said. "Are you sure that's going to hold?"

"You said you needed to move fast," Quee said. "And this was the best I could do on short notice."

A second, disreputable-looking alien had all three of

his arms deep inside the ship's influx tube, trying to wedge something out. After a moment, the creature removed the Clipsian scouting beacon. Quee walked over and took it in her hand, examining it.

"I never had any toys of my own," Quee said. "I had to play with things that I found. Junk tossed out from the floors above. This would have kept me entertained for hours."

With the repairs complete, Zachary, Ryic, Kaylee, and Quee climbed aboard the ship. Quee was carrying two shoulder bags, stuffed full with her belongings.

"Packing pretty heavy for such a quick trip," Zachary said.

"Oh, I'm not coming back," she said. "Sure, somebody might want me dead, but living all alone, below the bottom of Tenretni . . . I feel like I've already been buried."

Zachary took another look at Quee; he hadn't been expecting such a dramatic response, but she seemed sincere.

Ryic paid the two Tenretni mechanics, and once the boarding ramp ascended, the doors closed shut. Kaylee started the ship, and oxygen began to circulate. Zachary cautiously lifted his hand to where the hole had been and was relieved to find that the sealant was holding fast.

The four took their seats and fastened themselves in. As the buckler leaped into the sky, Zachary looked out the window and saw that Tenretni stood on the side of the desolate cracked planet Irafas. Unlike Earth, which was an oblate spheroid, Irafas looked like a broken eggshell, hollow on the inside with pieces of it missing. Giant mining shafts crisscrossed through its empty innards. It was a horrible, decaying place.

No wonder Quee wanted to leave.

0°

270°

90°

LIFE-FORM:
WUDAN

A NOMADIC SPECIES OF LIZARD-
LIKE ALIENS THAT SPREAD ACROSS
THE OUTERVERSE AFTER THE DE-
STRUCTION OF THEIR HOME PLANET,
WUDEBAR.

«THIRTEEN»

"That makes nineteen," Ryic said. "Only one question left."

"It's furry, gray, doesn't live on the ground, and eats worms," Zachary said, repeating the clues out loud. "I don't know. Is it a koala bear?"

"No," Ryic said. "It's a veildar gastropod!"

Zachary and Kaylee both sighed in frustration. Even Sputnik let out a groan.

"Ryic, you're supposed to think of things that everyone has heard of," Kaylee said.

"Who hasn't heard of veildar gastropods? They're the scourge of a thousand planets."

"Yeah, well, not Earth," Kaylee said.

While the others played twenty questions, another road trip staple of the Night family, Quee had been preoccupied with the Clipsian scouting beacon, taking it apart piece by piece and examining each nook and cranny as she did. She had become fixated on a square object that she had removed from inside the beacon.

"This must be the beacon's internal navigation system," Quee announced. "It has the entire manifest of where Nibiru's armada has been and where it's going."

"I don't care where the Clipsians are headed as long as it's not the same place as us," Ryic said.

"Then you should be sure to avoid Earth at all costs," Quee said.

Zachary and Kaylee both did a double take.

"What?" Kaylee asked. "That doesn't make any sense. It would be suicide for the Clipsians to attack Earth."

"Are you sure you're reading that correctly?" Zachary asked.

"The next location programmed into this beacon is your home planet," Quee said. "You can see for yourselves. The estimated arrival time is 13-721-863-55.21 ABB."

They all looked at her blankly.

"In Earth time, that's approximately three hours from now," Quee said.

"The Clipsians won't stand a chance against the IPDL," Kaylee said.

"Especially today," Ryic said.

"Why?" Zachary asked, having lost track of time. "What's today?"

"The Octocentennial, of course," said Ryic. "Starbounders from all across the outerverse will be at Indigo 8. Nibiru literally picked the worst possible day to stage an attack."

Kaylee thought for a moment. "Which would be counter to every strategic decision Nibiru's ever made as a general. What are we not thinking of?"

"Ryic just said it himself." Zachary's mind was racing. "If every IPDL officer and Starbounder in the outerverse is collected *on* Earth, what if they can't get *off*?"

"I'm not following," Ryic said.

"All of the starships are docked in the hangar beneath the Ulam," Zachary said. "If the officers can't get to them, they won't be able to launch into space."

Ryic still appeared confused. "What would be stopping them?"

"Giant iron doors," Kaylee said, catching on to Zachary's logic.

And she wasn't the only one up to speed.

"Say a cyber hack created a computer virus," Quee said. "One that activated the emergency defenses of a security system. Cerebella could be used to lock people *in* as opposed to locking them *out*. Earth would be helpless."

"That doesn't answer how someone was able to infect Cerebella with your virus," Kaylee said. "Only Director Madsen can grant access to the mainframe. And even then, humans aren't allowed inside, just aux-bots."

"If the Clipsians have been planning this all along, they must have had help from within Indigo 8," Zachary considered. "The accidents. The gravity failure in the Qube, the malfunctioning stun balls, the escaped vreeks.

What if they weren't caused by Cerebella, but by someone who wanted to *infect* Cerebella? What if someone was
using them as a way to get Madsen to okay an aux-bot
repair? An aux-bot already carrying the virus. The question is who."

"We have to warn Indigo 8," Kaylee said.

"What about hacking into the galactic bank?" Quee
asked.

"Change of plans," Zachary said, reaching for the lang-
link—but it was dead.

"Don't you remember what Doveling told us?" Ryic
asked. "There's no lang-link probe past the Asteroid
Curtain."

"Then we better speed up this ship," Zachary said.
"Where's the closest fold? We have to get to the other side."

"I'd take it easy on her," Quee said. "This buckler is in
no shape to be pushed."

But Zachary wasn't listening. He was already gesturing at the flight-deck window to accelerate. Kaylee was
spinning the Kepler cartograph, looking for the nearest
bend in space. She set some new waypoints, reorienting
the ship's path to Earth.

The buckler started rattling. It was feeling the strain of the extra speed, shaking as it moved toward the space fold.

"Even if you're right about the Clipsians attacking Earth, what does it have to do with us?" Ryic asked over the noise. "And why did someone want us dead?"

Zachary and Kaylee were both at a loss.

The ship made a final push for the fold and bounded through. Once it rocketed out the other side, they could see the Asteroid Curtain behind them. Zachary immediately turned back to the lang-link and sent a signal to Indigo 8. All that came back was static.

"I thought after we crossed the curtain our communications would be operational," Zachary said.

"They are," Quee said. "It's Indigo 8's that are down. The virus I created doesn't just infect the security system. It also temporarily disables all contact in or out of the site."

"Then we have to go back and warn them ourselves," Zachary said.

"And what do we do when we get there?" Kaylee asked. "All the ships will still be locked inside the hangar."

"Every virus has an antidote," Quee said. "If I can gain access to Indigo 8's mainframe, I can reverse it. But this ship has one more bound in it, tops. If you want to get back to Earth, we're going to have to find another ride."

All Zachary had to do was glance back at the metal plating covering the hole to know she was right. It was beginning to hiss loudly, and the last thing he wanted was a repeat of their previous landing.

"Where are we supposed to find a ship in the middle of the outerverse?" Ryic asked.

Not for the first time since they'd crash-landed on Sirocco, Zachary wished he knew where his brother was stationed on his Elite Corps mission. But of course it was classified, and Jacob wouldn't be dropping in anytime soon to save them.

Kaylee looked up from the Kepler cartograph.

"There is one person we could go to. Skold."

Zachary and Ryic looked at her like she was crazy.

"Cratonis is only one bound from here," she said. "If we can make it through that fold, we stand a chance."

"Who's Skold?" Quee asked.

"Just a galactic felon who held us hostage and tried to

sell us into slavery," Ryic said.

"You know what we call that on Tenretni? A friend."

Nobody was offering up any better ideas.

"Set the waypoints," Zachary said.

Kaylee punched them in, and the buckler headed for the next fold. Before they knew it, the ship was jumping again.

°°°

It was clear even from orbit that Skold was not a subtle salesman. Projected across the clouds floating above Cratonis in giant laser lettering was an advertisement. And although the alien language was illegible to them, the pictographs that accompanied it made it clear that Skold was selling ships and parts. If there was any question where Zachary and the others needed to go to find him, the large arrow pointing to a green spot on the moon's surface left no doubt.

"Bring her down easy," Quee said.

The buckler had survived the last leap, but just barely. Every light on the cockpit window was flashing, and the only thing keeping the metal plating from popping clear off the hole was Ryic's pressing his back and shoulder against it.

"This isn't going to hold much longer," he called, digging in his heels.

The ship was heading for the tip of the arrow, where a circular lawn served as a landing pad for incoming customers. Two other spacecraft were already sitting there. The buckler landed with a jolt, and the ship's rattling engine abruptly shut down.

Cratonis defied Zachary's expectations. When he had heard Skold describe his chop shop and the place he kept his stolen ships, Zachary imagined something dingy like Tenretni turned out to be or disreputable like the Fringg Galaxy Void Market. This was more like a park or a sculpture garden. There were small rolling hills with well-manicured grass that reminded Zachary of the fancy golf course he and his friends would sneak onto to sled during the winter. A large glass building sat on one of the hills, looking like it had been dropped there out of the sky. On the surrounding fields there were ships and machines of all sizes. Some appeared brand-new, others old and rusted. Four other customers were walking about, examining the inventory. Zachary, Kaylee, Ryic, and Quee began browsing as well.

It was still twilight, but the automated lampposts all around them began to blink awake. As they'd bounded across the outerverse from planet to planet, Zachary had stopped paying attention to day and night. In space it was hardly an accurate measure of time.

"Missed me already?" Skold emerged from behind a large vessel. He had cleaned himself up since they last saw him, having changed into a gray long-sleeved shirt and rubberized pants. The shockles on his ankles and wrists were long gone.

"We need a ship," Zachary said, foregoing any small talk.

"And here I thought you came to reminisce about all the good times we had together," Skold said. He glanced over to the landing pad and spotted the buckler. "Not much trade-in value. What else you got?"

"Access to my planet's galactic bank account," Ryic said. "And the Klenarog treasury."

"All right. Now you're talking," Skold said. "Let me show you some of the new merch."

He walked them over to a large, glossy ship.

"Oaxo luxury cruiser," Skold said. "Emperor-sized

hyperbolic sleep chambers, automated food materializer. Sail the outerverse in style."

"We need something with weapons," Zachary said.

"You planning on starbombing a planet?" Skold asked. "I didn't think the outerverse would corrupt you so fast."

"We're going back to Indigo 8," Zachary said. "We have reason to believe Nibiru and his Clipsian armada are planning to attack Earth."

"You sure you got your facts straight?" Skold asked. "Those charcs aren't exactly known for fighting battles they can't win."

"We're pretty sure they've found a way to lock down Indigo 8's starship hangar," Kaylee said. "All of the IPDL's greatest Starbounders will be there for the Octocentennial. They'll have no way of getting back into space. They'll be trapped."

"Leaving no one to protect Earth or the surrounding solar system?" Skold asked.

"Exactly," Zachary said.

"Come on, then," Skold said. "I've got a couple of pitchforks that are perfect for you."

He led them past the large glass building on the hill.

"Your house looks nearly identical to the Ulam at Indigo 8," Ryic said. Zachary was thinking the same thing.

"That's because it was the Ulam at Indigo 5," Skold said. "I forklifted it straight out of the ground." He gave a nod to a giant spaceship with enormous claws that Zachary had mistaken on first glance for a mountain. "One of my more inspired heists."

As they passed one of the large windows of the house, Zachary spotted three orange-and-black, one-foot-tall amphibious humanoids with long tails and webbed feet inside. One was pressing its lips up to the glass and blowing. Another was sticking out its tongue. The third was trying to pull the first two away from the window. Zachary remembered seeing the same tail and webbed foot in the glass jar housed within Skold's robotic outer shell. It was hard to believe the cutthroat criminal who had made so many enemies in the outerverse looked like *that* within his carapace. Zachary had seen dogs in his neighborhood that were more intimidating.

"I see you spotted the wife and kids," Skold said. "You don't think I do all of this just for myself, do you?"

Actually, Zachary did. Skold didn't exactly seem like a family man. But then, he didn't seem like an oversized orange-and-black newt, either.

Skold continued down the other side of the hill to a patch of grass where two used pitchforks were parked.

"You call those perfect?" Zachary asked. "They look like they've been sitting there for years."

"These are first gen," Skold said. "Trust me, they don't make 'em like this anymore."

"Probably with good reason," Zachary said.

"Said the kid wearing the hundred-and-fifty-year-old warp glove," Skold replied.

"That's my grandfather's glove you're talking about."

"Where's that battle-axe you took off with?" Kaylee asked, interrupting them.

"Already sold it," Skold said. "People like shiny, new things. They don't respect quality."

Zachary wasn't sure if Skold was being genuine or just a good salesman. Either way, they didn't have time to debate it.

"How much?" Zachary asked.

"For you guys, because we're friends, ten thousand serendibite."

Zachary knew they were being ripped off, but Ryic didn't bat an eyelash. So neither did he. Skold handed Ryic a small keypad, and after a few finger swipes the ships had been paid for.

Zachary, Kaylee, Ryic, and Quee stood outside the silver trident-shaped pitchforks. They would need to split up into pairs.

"Ryic, you come with me," Zachary said. "Kaylee, take Quee." Then he turned and addressed Quee directly. "Unless you want to go your own way from here."

"I've been going my own way for my entire life," Quee said. "I'm ready to try something different. Besides, you need me."

And it seemed that Quee took a certain amount of pride in that.

"Let me give you a few pointers on how to handle those things," Skold said. "They work a little differently than your average bounder."

"Look at that," Kaylee said. "You care about us after all."

"I just want to make sure you don't crash them into any of my other ships," Skold said. "Now, there's no autopilot.

It's all manual gesture recognition. There's still a standard Kepler cartograph, but you're going to have to hit the entry points on your own. For the command seat, left hand controls steering, right hand controls particle blasters. For the gunner, right hand, debris cannons; left hand, doppelform projectors. Positions can be flipped at any time."

"Sounds like you stole the instruction manual along with the ship," Kaylee said.

"It would be irresponsible not to," Skold replied.

"All right," Zachary interrupted. "We should probably get going."

Zachary and Ryic started for one of the ships; Kaylee and Quee went for the other. Skold reached out and stopped Zachary, taking hold of his wrist.

"Listen, kid, if you're going to keep trying to be the hero, you better quit thinking of that glove as your grandfather's, and start thinking of it as your own."

He let go of Zachary and stepped back.

"And by the way, you're probably going to need fuel, too," said Skold. "That's going to cost you extra."

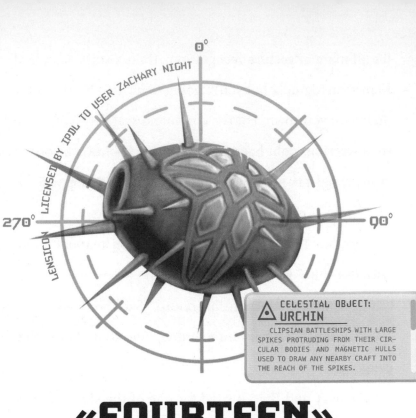

0°

270°

90°

⚠ **CELESTIAL OBJECT:**
URCHIN

CLIPSIAN BATTLESHIPS WITH LARGE
SPIKES PROTRUDING FROM THEIR CIR-
CULAR BODIES AND MAGNETIC HULLS
USED TO DRAW ANY NEARBY CRAFT INTO
THE REACH OF THE SPIKES.

«FOURTEEN»

Even though Zachary had logged some fly time on the way to Tenretni, piloting a buckler hardly compared to manning the controls of a pitchfork. It was kind of like learning to ride a motorcycle by practicing on your kid sister's trike. The snaillike pace of the buckler hadn't come close to preparing him for the whiplash speed of the ship he was now steering through the far reaches of space. Zachary's pitchfork whizzed ahead as he avoided the small planetoids drifting around a dwarf star that glowed dimly near the entrance to the fold.

Zachary was strapped into the command seat; Ryic was in the gunner's. They were able to communicate via short-range lang-links built into each cockpit.

"How's it hanging down there?" Zachary asked.

"Zachary, don't you know by now that in space there is no gravity? It is impossible for anything to hang. Things merely float."

"We're really going to have to work on your American slang," Zachary said.

Looking up through the cockpit window, he could see Kaylee piloting the other pitchfork. From Zachary's perspective, she was flying upside down, but here in the outerverse, where there was no top or bottom, Kaylee could have said the same thing about Zachary.

"What's our ETA to the next fold?" Zachary asked.

"Less than five minutes," Kaylee replied, her voice coming through the lang-link's speakers.

Zachary was eager to make this final bound. It would take them back to his own solar system, where he longed to see the distinct yellow light of the sun. His sun.

Zachary rotated his hands swiftly before the gesture-recognition sensor, sending his ship banking, avoiding contact with the hurtling space debris surrounding the dwarf star.

"According to that Clipsian scouting beacon, Nibiru's arrival outside Indigo 8 is imminent," Quee said over the lang-link. "By now, they will have already entered the solar system."

"Maybe we should find the nearest IPDL base," Ryic suggested. "See if we can't get some backup before making the jump."

"We don't have time," countered Kaylee.

"Facing an entire armada on our own?" Ryic asked. "It's just too big for us."

For a moment Zachary thought about agreeing. But then he gazed down at his grandfather's warp glove. He thought about what Skold had told him before they left Cratonis, about how this was no longer his grandfather's warp glove but his. It was true. It was time to forge his own legacy. He might not ever be as great as all the Nights who came before him, brilliant like his grandfather, or bold like his brother. But he could still become a hero. Or at least try.

"I'm not going to let Earth become another destroyed planet in the Outerverse Memorial. We can take them. Together," he said. "Star-bound and ready."

Kaylee's voice came over the lang-link next. "Star-bound and ready," she echoed.

Then there was a pause.

"Ryic, we're waiting on you, buddy," Zachary said.

"Star-bound and ready," Ryic said. "Although to be completely honest, I'm feeling more star-sick and ill-prepared."

"We all are," Zachary said, "but it's game on."

He steered his pitchfork into the space fold as the ship bounded for home.

° ° °

The two pitchforks emerged on the far side of Jupiter's orbit. Quee was right. The fleet of Clipsian attack ships—slicers and urchins—had arrived ahead of them. Hundreds were approaching Earth in the distance. Hundreds more were closing in on the Callisto Space Station, where the squadron of five IPDL pitchforks was still patrolling its perimeter.

"*This* was your plan?" Ryic asked. "Two against a thousand?"

"I never said it was a good one," Zachary replied.

"Well, if you want me to open Indigo 8's starship-hangar doors, I'm going to need access to Cerebella's mainframe," Quee said.

Zachary remembered what his lensicon had told him last time.

"Callisto handles all data storage and processing for Cerebella. Would you be able to override the virus from there?"

"If that's the closest I can get, I'll make it work," Quee said.

"Assuming those slicers and urchins don't blast Callisto out of the solar system first," Kaylee said.

Zachary looked ahead and saw that it was going to be a race to get to the Callisto space station. He steered his pitchfork straight for it. Kaylee was right behind him.

"I can't find the command to arm the cloaking shields," Ryic said.

Zachary typed in the air before him, and a message appeared on the cockpit window in response: THIS

MODEL DOES NOT COME EQUIPPED WITH ANY STEALTH TECHNOLOGY.

"Skold!" Zachary cursed under his breath.

There was nothing they could do about the pitchfork's shortcomings now.

"We're either going to have to outrun those Clipsian ships or face them head-on," said Zachary.

"I vote for option one," Ryic replied.

Zachary would have accelerated if the ship could have gone any faster, but it had already reached its peak velocity. He kept the pitchfork going in the straightest possible line, knowing that any deviation would decrease the ship's speed and delay their arrival at the space station. Though they were closing the gap with the slicers and urchins up ahead, it was becoming increasingly apparent that they were going to have to engage them in battle.

"There's no way we're going to make it there first," Zachary said.

"Well, at least we won't have to fight them alone," Kaylee said.

The squadron of IPDL pitchforks held their position even as the enemy continued its approach. The pitchforks were like a cavalry waiting to charge. That's what Zachary was hoping anyway. Because otherwise they were about to get slaughtered. Just when Zachary was sure he was going to see his allies destroyed, the five ships launched a synchronized attack of particle blasts and cannon debris at the slicers. A dozen of them were instantly obliterated. But the IPDL victory was short-lived. A second wave of Clipsian slicer ships swarmed the squadron like angry bees. Only instead of stingers, they used their razor-sharp blades to gash the trident-shaped spacecraft. Even with their silver-hued, reinforced hulls, the IPDL ships were diced to shreds. Two giant urchins swept in, magnetically pulling what was left of the pitchforks toward their spike-covered exteriors. The ships were skewered, punctured with so many holes that they crumbled apart.

"Okay, so maybe we will have to fight them alone," Kaylee said.

With Callisto's undermanned defense squadron wiped out, the Clipsian armada's distortion sensors seemed to have discovered the two additional pitchforks.

"Activating the doppelform projectors," Ryic said.

"Me, too," Quee said.

A pair of identical-looking pitchforks materialized on either side of the two original ships, making it appear that there were now six.

"Hold your fire," Zachary said. "No reason to give up our cover until we absolutely have to."

A cloud of slicers enveloped them and immediately began their assault. Two of the Clipsian ships attempted to sideswipe one of the doppelform projections, but rather than cutting through the steel hull of an IPDL pitchfork, they collided with each other, causing both to be severed in half.

Although the doppelform worked once, it would only serve as a temporary distraction. The Clipsians were able to deduce which ones were fakes by flying at all of them. A slicer nicked the back of Zachary and Ryic's pitchfork, and now that they'd been exposed, every other Clipsian ship would be trying to tag them next.

"Time for a new plan," Zachary said.

"Remember what we learned in flight class," Kaylee said. "Tactical turn left."

Zachary recalled the diagram their flight trainer had drawn on the electronic whiteboard during his lesson on tandem combat patterns. He initiated the maneuver, perfectly pulling off a gentle roll to the left alongside Kaylee. When surrounded by enemy combatants, tactical turn left was meant to disarm the adversary with an unexpected change of direction. The Clipsians seemed to be not only prepared for it, but one step ahead of them. They had cut off any path of escape.

"Tactical turn right," Kaylee said.

Zachary quickly gestured for his pitchfork to make an about-face, but as soon as the ship's prongs began to rotate, several slicers were countering the evasion tactic. One slammed the side of Zachary and Ryic's pitchfork, jolting Zachary forward in his seat. His nose smacked against the control panel, causing his eyes to water. The involuntary tears blurred his vision.

"Ryic, take over steering from your cockpit," he called.

"What?" Ryic asked. "I-I can't fly this thing."

Another slicer drove its blade into the pitchfork.

"Now!" shouted the still-blinded Zachary.

Zachary felt his ship lunge, and not in the graceful manner of an accomplished pilot. It twisted out of control, dipping violently. Slicers whizzed by the pitchfork without making contact.

"I'm getting hit from every side," Kaylee said over the lang-link. "I don't get it. I'm doing everything exactly by the book. Ryic, you need to do a three-point vertical climb."

Even through his clouded vision, Zachary could see that Ryic wasn't exactly pulling off the routine maneuver with finesse. The ship was ascending diagonally, making unpredictable moves every step of the way. But it was not Zachary and Ryic's pitchfork taking enemy blows. It was Kaylee and Quee's.

And then it hit Zachary.

"Kaylee, stop following IPDL protocol," he said. "Whoever betrayed us must have given the Clipsians the pitchfork flight patterns."

"Roger that," she replied.

Kaylee began to fly erratically as well, and it proved instantly effective. Slicer pilots seemed to be at a loss. The two pitchforks zigged and zagged their way closer to the Callisto Space Station.

Zachary's eyesight was coming back, too. Although he immediately wished that it hadn't. The first thing he saw was a black, prickly urchin heading toward them, its spikes looking even more deadly up close. And it didn't appear that Ryic's unintentionally bad piloting skills would save them from the ominous ship's magnetic pull. In fact, Zachary could already feel them getting sucked into its grasp.

"It's pulling us in," Kaylee said.

Quee unloaded a barrage of cannon debris at the urchin. The chunks of metal flew from the barrels of the pitchfork, but instead of damaging the enemy ship, they merely embedded themselves into the first layer of armor protecting the orb-shaped spacecraft.

The two pitchforks were being drawn closer to the spikes.

"We need to reverse course," Zachary said.

"I'm trying," Ryic said.

"The ship's too strong," Kaylee said. "There's no chance we're going to be able to get ourselves out of this."

"Not unless we figure out a way to turn off the magnetic pull," Quee said.

Zachary looked out through the cockpit window and could see the urchin pilot's charcoal skin glowing orange.

"I just might have a way to do that," he said.

"Get us out of this, and I'll do *your* laundry for a week," Kaylee said.

"Make it two," Zachary said.

Zachary's warp glove created a hole in space, allowing him to reach through. His hand, armed with a sonic crossbow, came out the other side of the hole, but he hadn't judged the distance appropriately. He came up a little short, still outside the urchin.

Zachary retracted his arm back through the hole and into his pitchfork. The magnetic pull was getting more powerful, and his ship was just moments away from getting turned into a shish kebab by the urchin's spikes.

He recalibrated his glove and opened another hole. This time, when his hand emerged it was inside the urchin's command deck. From the cockpit of the pitchfork, Zachary could see the Clipsian pilot react quickly. The alien reached out and grabbed Zachary's hand. Zachary had to hold on tight to the crossbow as the pilot tried to wrench it free. Zachary pulled away for a second, and it was all the time he needed to fire off a series of bolts. The round of sonic blasts reverberated throughout the cabin, knocking out the Clipsian and making impact with the enemy craft's control panel. The urchin's magnetic pull deactivated.

No longer trapped by the ship's unbreakable hold, Zachary and Kaylee immediately steered their pitchforks out of the way.

"Woo-hoo!" Ryic shouted.

"Just so you know, I like my T-shirts pressed," Zachary said for Kaylee's benefit.

"Don't make me wish I was killed by that urchin," Kaylee replied.

With no one helming the Clipsian ship, it tumbled into a pack of slicers, demolishing all of them. The urchin went spinning toward Jupiter, leaving the two pitchforks with a clear route to Callisto. In the distance it appeared that the alien armada was getting closer to Earth. If the hangar doors weren't unlocked soon so the IPDL ships could be released, Zachary's home planet would surely be destroyed.

"I'll take us in the rest of the way," Zachary said to Ryic.

They were about to make their final approach when

from above another urchin dropped into their path. The pitchforks were instantly caught up in the Clipsian ship's deadly pull.

"You gotta be kidding me," Zachary said.

He didn't hesitate, reaching out his warp glove to repeat the same trick as before. A hole opened in the urchin's flight deck, and Zachary's hand emerged with sonic crossbow in his grip. But the charcoal-skinned pilot swatted the weapon out of Zachary's glove. Zachary fumbled, trying to grab it before it was out of reach, but to no avail.

Zachary pulled his hand through the warp hole back into his own pitchfork.

"I lost the crossbow!" he shouted. "Kaylee, do something!"

The spikes of the urchin were coming at them quickly.

"I can't reach mine," Kaylee replied frantically. "It's in the storage compartment!"

Zachary braced himself as the tip of one of the spikes threatened to impale his cockpit window. But just before the piercing blow, the urchin was split in half as an IPDL battle-axe cracked the Clipsian ship open like a coconut, using its own sharpened blades. Zachary was elated. Backup from the IPDL had arrived. Yet it seemed there was only one of them.

"I'm starting to make a habit of saving your butts," said a voice over the lang-link. Zachary didn't recognize it at first. Then as he caught a glimpse of the battle-axe flying past, he saw who was piloting it.

Skold.

The alien fugitive was manning the very same craft they'd all shared on their way to the Fringg Galaxy Void Market.

"What are you doing here?" Zachary called back.

"I figured you guys could use some help," Skold said.

Zachary had suspected there was a part of Skold that was good, and he couldn't have picked a better time to show it.

"I thought you said you sold the battle-axe," Kaylee said.

"I lied," Skold said.

"Cover us until we make it onto Callisto safely," Zachary said.

"You got it," Skold replied.

The two pitchforks raced for the space station's open bay doors, as Skold blasted attacking slicers out of their way. Zachary steered his ship inside, landing roughly on a platform. Kaylee did the same.

Zachary unbuckled himself from his seat and retrieved a voltage slingshot from the cockpit's underbin. After the bay doors sealed shut, he exited and found that the station's environment recreated the gravity of Earth. Zachary took a moment, a *brief* moment, to suck in a deep breath. He was just happy to be alive.

Ryic, Kaylee, and Quee departed the pitchforks and joined him on the platform. Ryic and Kaylee carried sonic crossbows. Quee held a pair of robotic hacking hands. Sputnik sat on Kaylee's shoulder.

"All the emergency evacuation ships have been launched," Ryic said. "Callisto is empty."

"Not entirely," Kaylee replied.

She gestured her chin at a single IPDL pitchfork docked on the far side of the hangar.

"Right now, we just need to find that mainframe," Quee said, reminding them of why they were all here.

They ran to the iron doors leading into the hallway.

Zachary inserted his warp glove into the fist-sized indentation. But unlike the times before, this door didn't open.

"It's not working," Zachary said.

Quee slipped into her robotic hacking hands. She slid a thin metal rectangle the size of a credit card a quarter of the way into a barely visible slot below the indentation and began reading data off the exposed edge.

"Someone jammed the entry clearance," Quee said. "The previous glove imprint belonged to an IPDL officer. Someone named Excelsius Olari."

It took Zachary a second to realize that she was talking about Indigo 8's lone Clipsian resident: Professor Olari.

They had found their traitor.

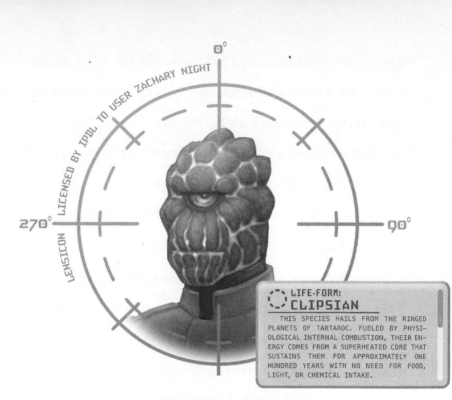

**LIFE-FORM:
CLIPSIAN**

THIS SPECIES HAILS FROM THE RINGED PLANETS OF TARTAROC. FUELED BY PHYSI-OLOGICAL INTERNAL COMBUSTION, THEIR EN-ERGY COMES FROM A SUPERHEATED CORE THAT SUSTAINS THEM FOR APPROXIMATELY ONE HUNDRED YEARS WITH NO NEED FOR FOOD, LIGHT, OR CHEMICAL INTAKE.

«FIFTEEN»

"The IPDL should really consider hiring a security consultant," said Quee. "A six-year-old with a stick of gum could break through this."

She punched a sequence of binary code into the same extended portion of the metal card sticking out from the slit. With a click, the iron door opened.

Zachary, Kaylee, Ryic, and Quee hurried into the long, white hallway. Zachary's mind was racing faster than his legs. How could he have been so naive about Professor Olari? Once they discovered that Nibiru and his armada were planning an attack on Earth, there should have been no question about who the saboteur was inside Indigo 8.

Zachary still couldn't figure out why they were targets, though. Maybe it had something to do with Kaylee's father or Zachary's parents or even Jacob. Could he have known something about Olari? Information he could have learned on one of his Elite Corps missions and passed on to Zachary? Or maybe it was something Zachary had witnessed in Professor Olari's morphology class.

Every question led to more questions. But Zachary didn't have time to put together all the pieces. He just knew they had to stop Professor Olari.

"The mainframe is located a half mile around the ring," Quee said, staring down at a map she'd apparently downloaded off the entry door's computer system.

"You realize there's a very good chance that Professor Olari already knows we're here," Ryic said.

Zachary and Kaylee readied their weapons. The group's footsteps echoed down the long hallway as they ran past room after room of abandoned scientific research. There were laboratories filled with test tubes still bubbling, refrigerator doors hanging open, and Bunsen burners left aflame. It was obvious that anyone working inside had fled.

Following the map, Quee led them to a junction point where the hallway split in three different directions.

"This way," she said, pointing to a staircase.

Quee began taking the stairs up to a platform three floors above. Once they reached it, they started down another circular hallway, which led to an open doorway.

"That should be the station's command center," Quee said.

As they got closer, Zachary could see through the open doors. Professor Olari was standing before a panoramic window overlooking Jupiter and the still-strong Clipsian armada orbiting it. Skold's battle-axe was blasting its way through more slicers.

Zachary and Kaylee moved to the front of the pack. Each took aim at Professor Olari as they entered the room. The Clipsian morphology professor slowly turned around.

"You're too late," Professor Olari said. "Everything's already been set into motion. Earth will be as barren as any other lifeless planet within the hour."

"You're wrong," Zachary said. "We're going to override the lockdown. Once those IPDL ships are freed, all of you Clipsians are going to be sent running."

"I highly doubt that," Professor Olari said.

He reached into his pocket and pulled out a photon pistol.

Zachary fired first, sending a lightning ball from his slingshot. But Professor Olari got off a shot of his own. A bright burst of light came at Zachary so fast he only had a millisecond to recognize this was most likely the end for him.

Yet the photon bolt didn't hit him. It was as if it didn't exist at all. Then Zachary realized that the electrical blast he had fired at Professor Olari had gone straight through him.

"Drop your weapons," said a voice from behind Zachary.

Zachary turned to find himself face-to-face with the barrel of a photon cannon. And the individual holding it was Loren.

Zachary let the voltage slingshot fall to the floor.

Kaylee released her grip on the sonic crossbow as well.

"I don't understand," Zachary said. "Why are you helping Professor Olari?"

"That's the thing," Loren said. "I'm not."

Keeping his photon cannon fixed on Zachary, Ryic, Kaylee, and Quee, Loren glanced at a thumbtack-sized device with an LED light on it, positioned on a nearby shelf.

"Cancel doppelform," Loren said.

The LED light went off and Professor Olari disappeared. Zachary's head was spinning. Then Loren kicked open an underbin at his feet, revealing Professor Olari bound and gagged inside.

"He hasn't been so cooperative," Loren said.

"*You're* the traitor?" Zachary asked. "The one who hired Quee to create the virus that locked down Indigo 8?"

"That's not the half of it," Loren said. "I'm the one who sabotaged the dreadnought and hired Hartwell to kill you."

"Why us?" Kaylee asked.

"That night in the laundry room," Zachary said. "Of course. You weren't washing those Chameleon jerseys. You were tampering with them. So they'd ignite during the game. And you were in the Qube when it malfunctioned."

"I couldn't risk having you expose me," Loren said.

"So you put my virus into the aux-bot to infect Cerebella," Quee said. "To initiate the lockdown."

"Nice work, by the way," Loren said. "You've got a real knack for programming."

"Your father's death," Zachary said. "You never intended to honor his legacy, did you?"

"No, I chose to avenge it," Loren said. "I told you. My mother said I could either get angry or be a hero. I guess now it's pretty obvious which one I picked."

"Your father wouldn't have wanted this," Zachary said.

"The IPDL stole him from me. Now they're going to pay for it."

"And all the innocent people on Earth?" Ryic asked. "What about them?"

Loren shrugged.

"They'll suffer the same way I did."

Loren pulled Professor Olari out from the underbin and removed the binding covering his mouth.

"I need you to translate something for me," Loren said.

He gestured to a small portion of the panoramic window, and a holographic display appeared showing another Clipsian. His charcoal outer layer was more cracked than that of any Clipsian Zachary had ever seen before, and his inner ember glowed brighter.

"Nibiru, I've handled the young Starbounders," Loren said. "There shouldn't be any more unforeseen disturbances."

Professor Olari stood there silently. Loren shoved the photon cannon into his back. Olari proceeded to translate, relaying the message to Nibiru.

Nibiru responded in the same off-planet Clipsian tongue.

"He says that the ships heading for Earth will be there within minutes," Professor Olari said.

"You would have been better off on that lava planet I redirected the dreadnought to crash into," Loren said.

"Technically it's magma," Ryic said.

"I think you just made the decision easy for me," Loren said. "I'll kill you first."

He pointed the photon cannon at Ryic. Just as he fired, Professor Olari lunged at him, taking the brunt of the blast and tackling Loren to the ground. Professor Olari grabbed hold of Loren's shoulders and slammed his head into the metal floor, knocking him unconscious.

Olari rolled onto his back, revealing a gaping photon wound in his chest. It went straight to his core.

"Quee," Zachary said. "Go. Now."

She ran over to the mainframe and began using her robotic hands to hack in. Zachary, Ryic, and Kaylee knelt around Professor Olari.

"Hang on," Zachary said. "We're going to get you out of here." But even as he spoke, Olari was fading.

"You must continue what I started," Professor Olari said, grabbing Zachary just above the elbow. "Armed with the knowledge I've left you, you can save the outerverse from an unspeakable evil. But share this information with no one."

Zachary felt Professor Olari's grip tighten and a burning sensation sear into his flesh. He pulled his arm back, wincing. Then Olari's eyes closed, and the superheated core inside his chest cooled to a lifeless gray. Any last sign of warmth was gone. It was that quick.

"What was he talking about?" Ryic asked.

"I have no idea," Zachary said, still smarting from the singed mark on his bicep.

"Almost got it," Quee said. Her fingers were back at work on the portion of the thin metal card sticking out of the mainframe.

Something caught Zachary's eye through the panoramic window. He watched as Skold's battle-axe flew so close to the glass that it looked as if the ship was going to crash right through it. But instead it turned and dipped out of view.

"I'm in," Quee said.

Zachary, Ryic, and Kaylee came up behind her.

"Okay," Quee said. "Communication lines are reopening. Lockdown is being reversed. And if you want, while I'm connected, I could make all the campus's drinking fountains dispense soda instead of water."

"Link us to Indigo 8," Zachary said.

Quee entered a command, and suddenly a holographic display appeared on part of the panoramic window. Dozens of IPDL officers were frantically hustling about in the command center of the Ulam, directing aux-bots to different parts of the control panels.

"Who is this?" one of the officers asked.

"My name is Zachary Night. Nibiru is leading an attack on Indigo 8. You need to get as many pitchforks out here as possible."

"The starship hangar is malfunctioning," the officer replied. "We've been trying to override the virus infecting Indigo 8 for the last couple hours."

"Well, you won't need to anymore," Zachary said. "We hard-lined into the mainframe from Callisto. Cerebella has been debugged."

"Then we'll initiate—"

Just then, the transmission cut off and all of the power inside Callisto started to flicker and hum.

"We must have been hit," Ryic said.

One by one, the bigger equipment panels began to shut down. Larger overhead lights flickered off around them.

Zachary looked out the window and spotted Skold's battle-axe as it flew past. Attached to its rear cargo hold was a trio of giant cylinders.

"What is Skold doing now?" Ryic asked.

Zachary fixed his lensicon's crosshairs on the device the battle-axe was hauling behind it. He blinked twice.

⚠ CELESTIAL OBJECT:
PERPETUAL ENERGY GENERATOR

THIS RARE AND HIGHLY VALUABLE ENGINE COMBINES FUSION, FISSION, AND VACUUM ENERGY TO ALLOW A CONTINUOUS FLOW OF POWER WITHOUT ANY EXTERNAL FUEL ADDED.

THE SECRET OF ITS MECHANICS IS TIGHTLY GUARDED BY A SHADOW ORGANIZATION OF SCIENTISTS KNOWN AS THE BLACK ATOM SOCIETY.

"He didn't come back here to save us," Zachary said. "He came to steal the perpetual energy generator!"

"Unbelievable," Kaylee said. "He knew Callisto would be unguarded. He used us again."

The display on the window started flashing the words *All-system failure.*

"We need to get out of here," Quee said. "Once the power goes down completely, every life-support system in the station will stop functioning."

"What about Professor Olari?" Ryic asked.

"He's gone," Zachary said.

The four started for the double doors. As the gravity in the space station faded, Zachary's strides became longer and lighter. Quee reached the hallway first. Ryic and Kaylee followed. But before Zachary could get through, the doors slammed shut. His nose smacked into a thick, circular glass window. Kaylee looked at him from the other side, confused. Then her eyes went wide, as if she saw something over his shoulder.

Zachary turned around just as a warp-glove-encased hand grabbed him by the hair and threw him across the room. He went tumbling. When he came up on his knees, he saw that Loren was pulling his own arm back through a warp hole. Loren's other hand was on a lever that must have manually shut down the doors.

"You're not going anywhere," Loren said. "Not without me, that is."

Loren bounced over to Zachary, the gravity getting so weak that his feet barely needed to touch the ground. Loren kneed Zachary in the chin, sending him flying backward. Zachary felt a shock of pain shoot straight through his teeth right up into his head. Loren used his warp glove to scoop up his fallen photon cannon, then aimed it at Zachary.

"I'm going to pilot my pitchfork out of here," Loren said. "And you're coming with me until I'm safely out of the galaxy."

Although they were standing ten feet from each other, distance didn't matter when you were wielding a warp glove. Zachary lashed out his own gloved hand, shooting it through a hole and grabbing the weapon Loren was brandishing. He tried to wrestle it free, but Loren struck back with his warp glove, reaching through a different hole and clutching Zachary's throat. Zachary spun out of the choke hold but had to pull his hand away from the photon cannon.

Even in the midst of the fight, he saw a hopeful sight through the panoramic window. The space fold from Indigo 8 had opened, and dozens of pitchforks and battle-axes were pouring out of it. He had no doubt they would fend off Nibiru's attack on Earth, even though it would be of little help to him now.

Callisto was beginning to feel the effects of the loss of power. The air had already grown stale, and the fans had stopped blowing. It seemed that there must have been something electric stabilizing the entire space station, because the structure was starting to crumble.

Kaylee, Ryic, and Quee remained locked outside the doors, watching through the glass window as Loren pounced again. He delivered a series of blows to Zachary's face and body before lifting him up and spinning him around. A coppery taste filled Zachary's mouth, and he knew it was from the blood pooling behind his teeth. Zachary felt the barrel of the gun jam into the small of his back.

"I'm going to open those doors and walk us out into that hallway," Loren said. "If you do everything I ask of you, maybe I'll let one of your friends live."

Zachary knew that once they walked through those doors, his friends would become casualties just like Professor Olari.

"I'll do whatever you want," Zachary said. "Just don't hurt them."

Loren pushed Zachary across the room toward the command center's control deck. As Loren reached out for the lever that would manually reopen the doors, Zachary seized the moment. He shifted his weight and grabbed hold of the photon cannon that had been pressed up to his back. He tried to rip it away, but Loren's fingers tightened. The two struggled to gain the upper hand on the weapon. They were at a stalemate.

"Did you think I'd really let you turn this gun on me?" Loren asked.

"No," Zachary said. "That was never part of the plan."

Zachary used all his muscle to aim the photon cannon down at the lever. Then his finger pulled the trigger. A beam of superheated light obliterated the entire lever and the control deck around it, leaving nothing but a gaping hole.

Loren put a hand to his head.

"What did you do?" he asked. "There's no other way out of this room."

The command center's walls were shaking vigorously now, and the panoramic windows were beginning to crack. Gravity was gone. Loren floated just above the smoking panel, shock turning to anger.

"You've killed us both," he said.

Yet Zachary looked remarkably calm.

He turned to the glass windows on the double doors

and called out to Kaylee and Ryic.

"Pull me through!"

With that, Zachary created a warp hole and stuck his arm in. His gloved hand emerged from a hole on the other side of the doors. Zachary could immediately feel fingers wrapping around his. Loren realized what Zachary was doing and squeezed the trigger on the photon cannon. The flash of light from the muzzle of the gun was the last thing Zachary saw before he was tugged into the warp hole itself.

While inside, he felt as if he was in between the fabric of space and time, where distance was nothing and time may or may not have been passing. Whether he was traveling through the hole for a fraction of a second or thousands of years, once he came out the other side, he was back with his friends.

Loren was at the sealed door in an instant, pounding his fists on the thick glass. But Zachary and the others turned their backs on him as he desperately started firing photon bolts at the reinforced door.

"The only way to get back to the pitchforks is the same way we came," Quee said.

Zachary pushed off, gliding through the long, white hallway that he had once run down. Ryic and Kaylee were having no problems keeping pace, but Quee was lagging behind, struggling to maneuver herself in zero gravity. Ryic stretched his arm and took hold of Quee's hand.

"Come on," he said. "I'll help you."

Wall panels were breaking loose and cracks were forming in the floor and ceiling below and above them. Tools and equipment from the neighboring rooms were now drifting through the thin air. Zachary spied a box of bio regulators moving past them in slow motion. He swam toward it and reached inside, pulling four masks out from the box. He kept one for himself and passed the other three to Ryic, Kaylee, and Quee. Zachary inserted his immediately and felt a rush of air reenergize him. Soon all four had the breathing apparatuses in their mouths.

Zachary reached the junction at the top of the staircase. The group was about to soar down the three flights of steps when they heard a loud crash. The far wall exploded open. A Clipsian slicer had smashed through the Callisto Space Station, tearing apart everything in its path: the walls, the stairs, the floors. Zachary and the others were just lucky they hadn't been crossing sooner, or they would have been in pieces, too.

The Clipsian ship went straight out the other side, leaving rubble and wreckage in its wake. Zachary could now see everything that was happening outside the space station. Pitchforks and battle-axes were annihilating the enemy fleet, facing down Nibiru's ships with superior speed and weaponry.

Quee pointed to the white circular hallway that led to the Callisto space hangar. To get there, they would have to cross a wide expanse littered with debris. There were chunks of staircase spiraling upside down, hovering platforms, and even metal rings floating in every direction. This was like the Qube's zero-gravity obstacle course times a thousand. But this was no race. Everyone had to get to the finish line.

Zachary gave a nod and pushed off, soaring past halogen tubes and pieces of dislodged banister. Springboarding off one of the staircases, Zachary propelled himself forward, leading the group to their destination. Or at least he thought he was, until Kaylee zipped past him. She gave him a satisfied smile. Ryic pulled Quee along behind them.

As they neared the other side, another slicer whizzed overhead, rolling to avoid the particle blasts coming from the pitchfork right on its tail. The Clipsian battleship's blades seemed so close, Zachary was surprised he didn't get a permanent haircut.

The group reached the circular hallway and raced all the way to the hangar, where they found their pitchforks, like everything else, beginning to drift away. Zachary and Ryic flew for their cockpit entrances. Kaylee and Quee did the same. They all took their seats and sealed themselves inside.

Without any power, the hangar doors weren't going to automatically open for them as they had when they arrived. Luckily, they had debris cannons. Zachary flipped a switch and fired, blasting the doors clear off.

Zachary removed the bio regulator from his mouth and activated the lang-link.

"Let's go back to Indigo 8," he said.

The two pitchforks zoomed out of the space station in time to see Nibiru's armada fleeing, heading away from Earth as fast as it could.

Zachary waved his gloved hand before the Kepler

cartograph, setting the waypoints for the fold between Io and Europa, the one that would take them back to the runway beneath the Ulam.

Once again his eye caught sight of the warp glove. This time as he looked at it, he couldn't help but think: while the glove had always fit him, now he fit the glove.

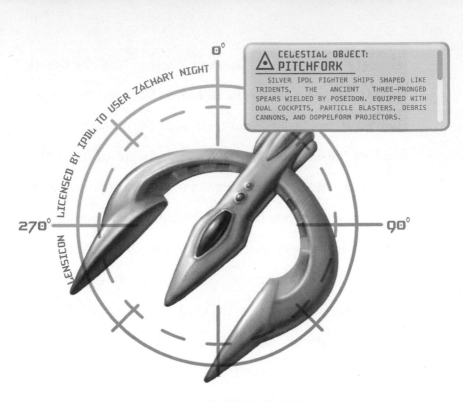

△ CELESTIAL OBJECT:
△ **PITCHFORK**

SILVER IPDL FIGHTER SHIPS SHAPED LIKE
TRIDENTS, THE ANCIENT THREE-PRONGED
SPEARS WIELDED BY POSEIDON. EQUIPPED WITH
DUAL COCKPITS, PARTICLE BLASTERS, DEBRIS
CANNONS, AND DOPPELFORM PROJECTORS.

«SIXTEEN»

Zachary was being led out of a debriefing room deep in the bowels of the Ulam. DiSalvo ushered him into the hallway, where Kaylee, Ryic, and Quee sat waiting on wooden chairs.

"I know that was a lot of questions in there," DiSalvo assured Zachary. "You must be exhausted."

It had been a whirlwind since they got back, filled more with precautionary procedures than fanfare or congratulatory hugs. As soon as Zachary and the others had landed their pitchforks in Indigo 8's starship hangar, they were met by a special team of IPDL officers dressed head to toe in protective suits. They were immediately taken to decontamination vaults to ensure there were no dangerous microbes on them, brought back from other parts of the galaxy. After being cleared, the next stop was the Ulam's infirmary, where Indigo 8's emergency-medical-assistance team injected Zachary and Kaylee with doses of vitamin serum and placed them in warm baths of gelatinous liquid. Ryic and Quee were sequestered in separate rooms to be given special treatments unique to their off-planet physiology.

The only permanent injury Zachary had received was an oddly shaped pattern of burns branded into the skin on his arm where Professor Olari had grabbed him. The medical team had tried to treat it with salves and ointments, but it seemed Zachary would be living with it for the near future.

Once all their vitals were checked and rechecked, the four of them were brought to the debriefing room, where they were individually questioned by a committee of IPDL intelligence officers about their time in the outerverse. Zachary had been the last to sit before the committee. Now he was rejoining his friends in the hall.

"Not exactly the hero's welcome I was expecting," Zachary said.

"Was it just me, or did that guy who wouldn't come out of the shadows give you the creeps, too?" Kaylee asked.

"Definitely not just you," Zachary said.

One of the inquisitors had remained hidden in the corner of the room. It was the same masked figure they had seen exiting Madsen's office before he punished them with freighter duty.

"And what was with all those questions about the Black Atom Society?" Ryic asked. "I've never even heard of it."

"After all the talk about Nibiru and how he got away, the only thing they really seemed to want to know about was the perpetual energy generator," Quee said.

"You're right," Zachary said. "I even got the feeling they thought we were working with Skold."

"The whole thing was weird if you ask me," Kaylee said.

Henry Madsen approached from the other side of the

hall, looking relieved. It was the first time they had seen him since their return.

"I want you to know that I take full responsibility for what happened to you," Madsen said. "We're still trying to figure out how Loren sabotaged the dreadnought's starbox and got those felons onto the ship. You must know that this was not the punishment I had intended when I sent you on that freighter. But with the way things turned out, I guess it was most fortunate that I did."

Zachary couldn't help grinning with pride.

"Humankind will never know that it was on the brink of destruction today," Madsen continued. "And they'll never know that if it weren't for you, this planet we call Earth would be gone."

Madsen led the group down the hall to the large open platform, and they all stepped inside. It began rising up.

"Professor Olari gave his life to save us," Zachary said.

"I would have expected nothing less from him," Madsen replied. "Did he give you anything before he passed? Anything at all?"

"No, sir," Kaylee said.

Zachary and Ryic concurred. But then Zachary

glanced down at the burn marks on his arm. It almost appeared as if they had formed a grid of blackened squares, just like the tattoos he'd seen on the knuckles of Quee's hacking hands. Zachary thought perhaps Professor Olari *had* given him something before he died. He was about to tell Director Madsen when he remembered what Olari had said: not to share this information with anyone.

Sputnik peeked his head out from Kaylee's pocket.

"I hope you're not planning on bringing that to any bonfires," Madsen said.

"I thought maybe he could live with me," Kaylee said. "You know, as the Lightwing girls SQ's pet."

"I'll see what I can do."

The platform arrived at the ground floor of the Ulam. Zachary saw his mom and dad sitting on a bench waiting for him. He was running into their arms as they stood up.

"Mom, Dad," Zachary said.

"Thank God you're alive," Zachary's mom said.

Through their tight squeeze, Zachary could see that Ryic and Quee were standing off to the side with Madsen, while a plainly dressed, sweet-looking woman held Kaylee close. He couldn't help overhearing.

"I know your dad wanted to be here," Kaylee's mom said. "He got stuck doing some business in the Tranquil Galaxies."

"That's okay, Mom," Kaylee said. "I understand."

Kaylee's mom looked at her, surprised.

"Wait," she said. "That's it? You're not upset?"

"No. In fact, I have a whole new appreciation for what Dad does."

Zachary's dad stepped back and got his first good look at the cuts and bruises on Zachary's face. His mom finally released her grip on him.

"If I had lost you, I don't know what I would have done," she said.

"I'm okay," Zachary said. "Really."

Zachary's mom gave him a soft smile that seemed to say she was okay, too.

"You should see what I can do with this glove now. I've gotten pretty good at it."

"Just like your brother," Zachary's dad said. "A warp-glove whiz."

"I think I'm finally worthy of the Night name," said Zachary.

Zachary's mom looked into his eyes and put her hands on his shoulders.

"Zachary, you didn't need to do something heroic to be a Night. You just needed to be yourself."

Suddenly Zachary felt a weight lift off his shoulders. It was as if he were floating in space.

○ ○ ○

Zachary tugged on the rudder of a solar sailboat, causing it to tilt on its side. Ryic clung to the railing for dear life as the boat zipped across the windless lake. Zachary eyed the enormous translucent sail catching the rays of sunlight that powered the boat forward at breakneck speed.

"Watch out, crossing your bow!" Kaylee called out from another boat.

She and Quee were cutting them off, blocking their light and scraping alongside them as they passed.

"I never should have let you guys talk me into this," Ryic said.

"Relax," Zachary said. "Quee hacked the doppelform generator. Anyone looking will find the four of us study-ing in the Skyterium. Besides, what's the worst that could happen? Madsen sends us all off on custodial duty again?"

Zachary tacked, flipping the sail to the opposite side of the boat and turning the rudder. Now he was charging toward the final buoy, just a length behind Kaylee.

"What do you say we make this extra interesting?" Kaylee shouted back at Zachary. "Not only does the loser do the winner's Celestial Physics homework for the week, but let's throw in that Outerverse Languages report, too."

"You're on," Zachary said.

The two solar sailboats raced for the finish line, nose to nose.

"Aw, come on," Ryic cried. "No more bets!"

"Get used to it, buddy," Zachary said with a smile. "The year's just getting started."

STARBINDER
OF TERMS

asteroid prison: a remote location used to house the most dangerous intergalactic felons in the outerverse.

aux-bot: a maintenance robot used for planetary and off-planet repairs.

battle axe: a large IPDL starship named for the sharpened metal blades protruding from its hull.

Battle of Siarnaq: a famed intergalactic battle in which a small Starbounder battalion defeated over a thousand Clipsians under Gerald Night's (Zachary Night's grandfather) command.

Binary Colonies: outerverse settlements inhabited by sentient robots.

Black Atom Society: a secret scientific organization with ties to the Callisto Space Station.

buckler: a small, defensive starship used by IPDL security forces.

Callisto Space Station: an IPDL research facility hidden among the moons of Jupiter.

Cerebella: the hyperintelligent mainframe computer that runs all of Indigo 8.

Chameleon: a Capture the Flag–style game played at Indigo 8.

charc: a slang for Clipsians in reference to their charcoal-colored skin.

clairvoyant: a star vessel used for galactic safaris, optimal for sightseeing due to its external glass pods.

Clipsian: an alien species fueled by internal combustion; while most are peaceful, the more aggressive tribes have ravaged hundreds of defenseless populated planets.

com-bot: robots used for battle-training exercises and combat sport.

Cometeer: a third-year trainee at Indigo 8.

Cratonis: a planet beyond the Indigo Divide where Skold resides.

Darkspeeder: a fourth-year trainee at Indigo 8.

debris cannon: a projectile weapon found on pitchforks that fires junk at high speed.

dehydra: a giant Siroccan beast that uses its nine siphon tendrils to absorb water from its victims.

Desultar Prospecting Station: a mining facility located

in the path of a gravity sinkhole.

distortion sensor: a device used to identify cloaked or camouflaged ships.

doppleform: a holographic simulation of either an individual or a starcraft.

dreadnought: a large IPDL starship used for transporting heavy loads.

Elite Corps: a classified, top-tier Starbounder subdivision sent on covert missions.

extraction: a banned interrogation technique that uses needles to remove memories directly from the subject's brain.

Flobian roach brain: a favorite Klenarogian snack.

friction boots: footwear used in zero-gravity situations to enable its user to temporarily stick to surfaces; also known as Armstrongs, in honor of the man who first walked on the moon.

Fringg Galaxy Void Market: an illegal black-market trading hub.

galactic fold: a wormhole that connects distant points in the galaxy, allowing starships to travel through the infinite outerverse.

greebock: common space cattle.

hopper ship: a small spacecraft used to travel short distances and not equipped to travel through interdimensional folds.

human carapace: a robotic outer shell used to house non–human beings.

Indigo 8: Earth's IPDL training facility, hidden in the Adirondack Mountains.

Indigo Divide: the boundary where IPDL-protected space ends.

Inter-Planetary Defense League (IPDL): a coalition formed to keep peace throughout the outerverse that is made up of disparate but peaceful intergalactic races.

Kepler cartograph: a map of every known galactic fold in the outerverse; named after Johannes Kepler, the famed mathematician and astronomer.

Kibarat: a domed farming planetoid that travels between galaxies like a comet.

Klenarogian: a humanoid, super-elastic species from the planet Klenarog.

lang-link: the outerverse equivalent of radio communication.

lensicon: a contact lens with instant image recognition, allowing users to identify whatever they are looking at.

Lightwing: a first-year trainee at Indigo 8.

magnetic grappling hook: a device used to traverse the outside of a spaceship during an untethered space walk.

magnetic tweezers: an all-purpose device with a tendency to accidentally emit neutron bursts.

off-planet bio regulator: the outer space equivalent of an oxygen tank.

outerverse: the entirety of the cosmos.

particle blasters: a starship weapon that fires super-charged atoms at its intended target.

Pele 9: a lava planet located in the Desultar Nebula.

perpetual energy generator: a device with near-infinite power used to run the Callisto Space Station.

photon bow: a weapon similar to a regular bow, except instead of arrows, it fires superheated light.

pitchfork: a Starbounder's standard-issue fighter ship, shaped like a trident, the ancient three-pronged spear wielded by Poseidon.

Qube: Indigo 8's zero-gravity practice chamber.

serendibite: clear cubes of black sand—the standard outerverse currency.

shockles: electrically charged handcuffs.

Sirocco: a salt planet, entirely barren and lacking any water, in the Desultar Nebula.

skyterium: the top floor of the Ulam, whose entire roof acts as an enormous telescope.

sleeping quarters (SQ): the name given to the cabins where Starbounders sleep.

slicer: a Clipsian combat ship named for its razor sharp edges.

sonic crossbow: a handheld weapon that fires beams of sound.

Sputnik: Kaylee's pet vreek, named after the first Russian satellite sent into space.

spaste: flavored space food; roughly the size of a tube of toothpaste, spaste contains enough sustenance to keep an individual alive for days.

starbox: the brain of a starship, roughly the size of a deck of playing cards.

starchery: the art and technique of shooting a photon bow.

stun ball: an electrically charged device that can immobilize an individual for hours.

sweat mite: a moisture-hungry space parasite.

Tenretni: a tiered city located beyond the Indigo Divide, on the broken planet of Irafas.

Tranquil Galaxies: a region of the outerverse ravaged by Nibiru's Clipsian army.

Ulam: Indigo 8's main building, home to everything from the skyterium, at its very top, to the space hangar, on its lowest underground level.

urchin: a Clipsian battleship with large spikes and a magnetic hull.

voltage slingshot: a handheld weapon that fires electrically charged ammunition.

vreek: a sluglike organism native to the tundra planets that seeks out heat to reproduce.

warp glove: an IPDL tool that opens folds in space and allows its user to extend his or her reach over vast distances from a stationary position.

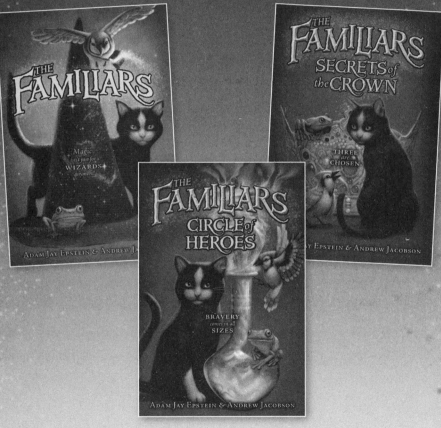